IN THE TIME OF THE SULTANS

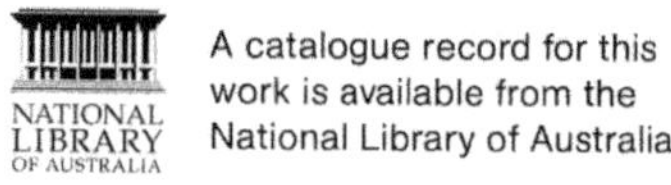

First published in Athens, Greece © 1965 by Panos N. Tzelepis

Publication authorised by the Tzelepis family

Front cover image courtesy of the Getty's Open Content Program: *Market of Eminonu Square and New Mosque/Yeni Cami*, Istanbul, 1884-1900, Sébah & Joaillier. Pierre de Gigord Collection of Photographs. The Getty Research Institute, 96.R.14

ISBN: 978-0-646-83959-2

Published by Cycladic Press, Sydney, Australia

https://cycladic-press.com/

IN THE TIME OF THE SULTANS

Urban Chronicles From 19th Century Istanbul

PANOS N. TZELEPIS

Translated by
CHARLES HOWARD

Contents

Introduction

Panos N. Tzelepis (1894 Constantinople—1976 Athens) belongs to the generation of Greek scholars and intellectuals known in Greek social and cultural history—and especially in literature—as the "Thirties Generation" or the generation of the interwar period. This includes the Nobel Prize-winning poet George Seferis and the architect Dimitris Pikionis—whose remodelling of the environs of the Acropolis in Athens is marked by his aesthetic acumen—and other important writers who depicted Greek society in their works and who, in their own way, educated the public about modernism and realism. At the same time, they promoted the idea of "Greekness," a notion which connects Greeks with their place and lineage in history.

After his studies in Istanbul, Athens and Paris, Panos Tzelepis (also written as Djelepy) established himself in Greece where he made significant contributions as an architect, guided by his Western education and the modernist movements of the first half of the 20th century.[1] He also held deep respect for vernacular architecture and artistic expressions found in the works of simple folk whose knowledge was handed down to them by previous generations. He left behind studies on Greek vernacular architecture as well as public buildings for children, educational institutions and sports facilities.

Tzelepis is renowned as an architect whose work took into account the human person and its specific needs, in combination with the harmonious use of materials. Throughout his life he was also involved in writing and translation. It is known from his notes that he had translated the entire poetic oeuvre of Charles Baudelaire into Greek, a life-task, as he described it, which unfortunately has not been found amongst his personal effects. A book of his poems published in 1966 in Athens testifies to a man who knew how to handle language in a measured, simple and beautiful way as much as he handled the materials of his architectural craft.

At an advanced age, having retired from architecture and his many other cultural activities, Tzelepis devoted himself to writing a number of stories which he published in two books. The current book, *In the Time of the Sultans*, was first published in 1965 in Athens, and the second, *The Story of a Daïs*,[2] was published in 1971. These stories are set in Istanbul/Constantinople in the late 19th and the first two decades of the 20th century, that is until the overthrow of the Ottoman state and its transition into the modern republic of Turkey. This is the period during which Panos Tzelepis was born and grew up, a period whose events he was very familiar with as he lived in Constantinople until the age of 20. He commenced his first studies there, which later shaped him into an architect who followed in the footsteps of his accomplished father, the architect Nikolis Tzelepis (1823—1906).

Nevertheless, when the time came for him to tell us about something other than architecture and its sociological and psychological dimensions, Tzelepis wanted to talk about the people who in their own way defined the life and times of his birthplace of Constantinople. This was a world which by that point no longer existed, forever lost to history due to World War I and the enormous geopolitical changes it brought about, drastically altering the lives of people in that era.

Panos Tzelepis's preface to this book tells us with the precision of the technical professional that he was, the reason why he decided to record the lives and times of these people, as well as how he made use of his source material. His material consisted of the living narratives of Stavris, his personal narrator, a relative, associate and friend of his. Stavris was a man who was born and grew up in the second half of the 19th century in Constantinople, and who died of hardship in Athens in 1940 during the war. Stavris recounted these stories to him as an old man, just as Tzelepis too was of an advanced age when he finally decided to publish them, preserving these chronicles for posterity. We can assume that these stories spent some time in written form before finally making it into print.

In these stories—none of which resemble each other apart from the literary style used by Tzelepis—we read about ordinary people, workers, small businesspeople and craftspeople of both the neighbourhood and the port. They are stories about life outside the home, away from the household and the family unit. The world of Stavris is the world of the street and is consequently exclusively male. This is also a world that frequently existed on the margins of legal life.

The smuggling of tobacco and hashish, severely prosecuted by the Ottoman authorities with special units, created a scenario in which the people involved in it, often as a side line to their legal work, clashed with the authorities. These confrontations and pursuits, with failures and successes on both sides, was a game of survival, disobedience, daring, courage and challenge, and also shaped a class of people that cut across all ethnicities living in Constantinople at that time. These were the people designated as *daïdes*, or *kabadaïdes* (from the Turkish word *kabadayı*), who had developed their own codes of honour, conduct, justice and at times undertook the protection of vulnerable social groups and individuals. These people are scattered throughout the short stories contained in the present book, along with other emblematic figures, such as a Jewish doctor who treated the poor; an old Persian man, Bechlioul-Aga, who transformed his tea-house into a dormitory every night for the homeless; a thinker and amateur philosopher, Sofu-Hadji-Thomas (The Wise Pilgrim Thomas) and old Hadji-

Minas (Minas the Pilgrim) who operated a famous yet discreet *teke* or hashish den—among other characters.

In the book *The Story of a Daïs* (1971), which we hope to see republished in Greek but also in English translation at some point, Tzelepis deals with one personality only—Daï-Andris—and writes of various events from his life and milieu, also recounted by Stavris, who is younger than Andris and in a sense his follower. Standing out amongst these stories is the novella "The End of a Contraband," about a major tobacco, hashish and cigarette smuggling operation from one end of Constantinople to the other, that is from the Asian territory of the city to the outskirts of its great European centre. Stavris—who Panos Tzelepis carefully listened to, faithfully conveying his stories—must have been a charming storyteller; it is clear that Tzelepis conveyed his voice, with its many Greek and Turkish words and expressions, exactly as he heard them from Stavris. Nevertheless, Tzelepis, despite modestly declaring in his preface that he does not claim the title of a writer, is himself a charming narrator, keeping the reader riveted to the narrative, just as in life he was regarded as a charming person.[3] Scattered throughout his stories are also excellent topographical descriptions that serve as historical documents of Istanbul, which we boldly suggest bears an amazing resemblance to its present appearance, despite the hundred years that have passed since then.

These people and their stories, as Tzelepis tells us, belong to a time lost forever, a world of yesterday. However, their world-views, behaviours and ways of life have also been preserved in another cultural heritage that brings them alive for us today. Here we are talking about the *rebetika* songs,[4] and the world in which they were born, sung and disseminated. The personal characteristics of *mangia* (grit/bravado)—exemplified in both good and bad behaviours, authentic and inauthentic expressions, a code of honour that is both followed and transgressed—are among the many things which the old *rebetika* songs describe, and which comprise the spirit that emerges through the stories of Stavris, immortalised and gifted to us by Panos Tzelepis.

— *Niki Stavridi*

English translation : *Anastasia Caramanis*

---

1. On the architectural oeuvre of Panos N. Tzelepis there is an unpublished doctoral dissertation (1983) by National Technical University of Athens professor Nikos Holevas (1944-2015).
2. An approximate translation for the word "daïs" is "street tough."
3. This is based on what was said about Tzelepis from people who knew him. There are also works by artists who depicted him in paintings, as well as a bust held in an art gallery on the Greek island of Tinos.
4. Urban folk songs, originally composed and disseminated in Greece (Piraeus, Athens, Thessaloniki), and also brought by refugees from Asia Minor, after the war of 1919-1922 and following the destruction of Hellenism there.

Στὴ μνήμη
τοῦ ΚΩΣΤΗ

Prologue

Stavris is not an imaginary character. He was a relation of mine, a colleague and friend too. He was born in Sinem Köy in 1866. His father, a very conservative person, said he was unruly and the two never lived in harmony. For that reason, after Stavris's mother died, he left his father, his home and his two brothers. He longed to become a sculptor, but the school of life, which he threw himself into at an early age, made him a marble mason.

By nature a follower of Epicurus, he made friends with easy-going types and free-spirits and frequented taverns and bordellos. However, he did not neglect his home life and was gifted with natural charm and talents. From the ages of 27 to 31 he was one of the best known "*daïdes*" or "bullies" in Constantinople. Known as "Stavris the Stonemason" to the Greeks and "Taşçı Stavri" to the Turks, he was loved by all for his forthrightness and bravery. This was a time when the practice of "*daïliki*" was considered by the ordinary people, and *was* in fact a mission of justice which protected them, without distinguishing between races.

His life changed in 1897 when he fell passionately in love with an older Turkish woman. If her people had discovered this, religious and racial fanaticism would have condemned them to a terrible death. To escape from this doomed love and to save his beloved's life, he joined the Greek Army as a volunteer in the War of 1897. His fate ordained that he would be badly wounded, would recover and be relieved of all that had weighed upon him up until then. The horrors of war taught him a lot and he returned to Constantinople a changed man. He became a marble contractor, honest and capable in his work, and for that reason much loved. Stavris died in Athens at the age of 76 from the hardships of the German occupation.

He told his stories to me during the peaceful years of his old age, recalling times past. They are incidents from the lives of humble people, the lives of other *daïdes* and from his own life; told exactly as they were lived by those who, without suspecting it, gave a special character to the New Babylon that was Constantinople towards the end of the nineteenth century. A time of prosperity for some, but one also ravaged by the bloody struggles between races that made up the declining Ottoman Empire; struggles that were orchestrated by the Great Powers, the so-called "Christian" ones, so that they could later interfere "peacefully" by imposing sanctions that drained both the country and its people. Despite these criminal schemes they did not manage to corrupt the intrinsic virtues of ordinary people to the point that they lost their humanity. This is a fact demonstrated by the contradictory aspects of these peoples' feelings, when bad deeds committed out of anger were often accompanied by behaviours suggesting regret or remorse. This shows that when people are not influenced by political intrigues and religious fanaticisms they know how to live together in amity.

Having kept faithful notes of his reminiscences, I am now bold enough to publish them without any literary embellishment, simply with the hope that these chronicles of times past, in a place which has changed radically, may still be of interest. If even one reader can be found, I will be as happy as the Persian poet, Sheik ul Reis, who shouted happily in the marketplace one day:

"A fellow being has recited some of my verses! Thanks be to Allah that they didn't go to waste!"

— Panos N. Tzelepis
Athens, 1965

ONE

The Brawl of the Daïdes

One dawn, Daïs-Andris was sitting in the yard in front of his shop slowly drinking his morning coffee. Suddenly, from the opposite corner of the alley another *daïs* appeared, Miltos the Bull, a big, muscular man of about fifty. His dark red hair—bushy and upright—grew low on his forehead. His eyes, set deep beneath thick brows, played quickly here and there as if he were scouting his surroundings. His wide moustache moved upwards every now and again as though his lips were trying to relieve themselves of the weight. This had become a tic and was accompanied by heavy breathing through the nose. He walked with a hip-swaying stride, weighing each step and swinging his long arms slowly, his head thrust slightly forward, ready to rush at any appearing enemy. All this gave Miltos the appearance of a human beast. In truth, he was strong as a beast, and without boasting, a truly brave man, by profession a tobacco smuggler. He always kept his word and was good-hearted and generous, especially to the poor. Nobody had any grievances with him, except the agents of the "Regie," the tobacco monopoly, who feared him; as did the police, who let him go about his business without much harassment, just enough to make a show; though they did submit constant reports about his activities and he had some twenty charges pending. But Miltos the Bull knew how to reward the coppers, sometimes with high quality tobacco which they—poor as they were—especially appreciated.

He lived outside the city in the hills and plains and was known to go on foot as far as the mouth of the Bosphorus at the Black Sea, seven hours walk away. His hideouts were in the tobacco villages. Sometimes he made an appearance in the village he came from, though none of his family still lived there. He brought down to the city whole loads of tobacco hidden in crates under fruit and vegetables and picked his helpers from among the most able and fearless young men, one of whom gained great fame: Leonis from the tobacco village of Ay-Yiorgi, who was greatly feared in the prisons. As the song went: "Break open the prison walls so Leonis can pass."

Every now and again, the two of them, Andris and Miltos, had their differences and clashed. Not over their business, but over women. Both were sought after as lovers and managed their affairs as they wished. With their fame, their feats and their style, they had plenty of women at their disposal, of all races and types. They had only to extend their hand to reap the fruit. At that time, there was friction between them because some of the more romantic of the women wanted to enjoy the love of both at the same time, causing trouble for the two *daïdes* and making them fall out.

The Bull passed by without greeting Andris, who took it as a great insult.

"Hey loser," he shouted, "don't you say Good Morning?"

"Go to hell you lazy cur!" roared Miltos the Bull.

That did it. Andris rushed into the shop and grabbed his weapon, a large club he had inherited from his father who was a night-watchman. When he came back into the yard, he found the Bull waiting for him opposite the shop. As soon as the latter saw the club, he pulled out the knife he always kept hanging at his left side under his jacket. He stood outside a small, low roofed grocer's shop, ready for the fight. They were wild with anger and breathing heavily. When Andris saw Miltos waiting for him, he paused, "Come further out you hamal," thundered the Bull.

"Go on, get out of here you animal and don't make me cover myself in blood first thing in the morning," answered Andris scornfully.

Miltos switched his knife to his left hand, extended his right arm to the low roof of the grocer's shop, tore loose a tile and hurled it at Andris. The latter kept cool, grabbed the tile out of the air and sent it spinning back straight at the Bull; he ducked, and the window of the grocer's shop shattered. Miltos wrenched off another tile and hurled it with even more force at Andris, who again managed to grab it and send it back at the Bull. This strange combat with tiles used as missiles lasted some time with oaths accompanying every throw. They called each other scabs, lost souls and so on, but nothing that would really offend their honour, nor anything coarse about each other or their families, or their lovers. They blew and roared like dragons. People had gathered round to watch from a distance this unprecedented battle of the two *daïdes* whose roaring and the din of smashing glass and tiles disturbed the peace of the cool morning.

No one dared to intervene, not one movement, not one word. Only the grocer, a short, stout *karamanlis*, watching with agony the tiles of his shop disappearing and the windows smashing, dared for one moment to approach the Bull and whimper hesitantly, "Daïs Milto, my child, you'll destroy a poor man's shop."

Miltos the Bull, as if he had suddenly become aware of something bad going on, stopped short and looked strangely at the grocer, "I'll pay for everything you cry baby, don't worry."

And then, like two beasts sated by an inconclusive battle, the two *daïdes* both stopped at once. It was as though each had silently acknowledged the other's strength. Miltos the Bull returned his knife to its sheath under his jacket, gestured disdainfully with both hands at Andris, wiped his palms together to remove the dust, gave a sideways glance at the shop and another at the grocer, and left, walking heavily and moving his arms in a circular motion as if to clear the way for his giant-like body. Andris, in the yard, made a scornful gesture as if getting rid of something bad and roared, "Go on, get lost you son of a bear!" He banged the club down onto the iron table, sat down heavily on a stool, lit the cigarette he had stuck behind his ear and continued to drink his coffee as if nothing had happened. One or two of the spectators made as if to approach him, while others watched Miltos the Bull as he left cheerfully. Andris shouted loudly, "Go on all of you. Get to your work." He wanted no praise for himself, nor any criticism of the Bull.

The same day a Persian turned up with a donkey-load of tiles for the grocer and a Jewish glazier came with a case of glass panes and a team of men to fit them. No other damage had been done to the grocer's shop. Andris watched the repairs opposite from the shop, stroking his moustache and feeling satisfied both with his fellow Daïs-Miltos and with himself.

TWO

The Girl From Turbot Creek

One day in April I was alone at the foundry. Master-Markos and two others, the craftsman and his helper, had gone to deliver a finished piece. The other craftsman hadn't come into work that day and his apprentice had taken the opportunity to slip off and while away his time who knows where. It was past noon; I had eaten and rested for a while, drinking my sweet boiled coffee at the little coffeehouse in the Lane of the Foundries. I hadn't been back at the shop long when the room suddenly darkened. At first, I paid no attention, but soon it made my work difficult. It was as if something had been placed in the entrance to stop the light coming in. I turned around and looked towards the door, which was the only opening.

In the dim rays of light stood a strange silhouette: a woman in a long skirt, very wide at the bottom. Her arms were extended, resting against the arch of the door; you'd say she was trying to prevent somebody from leaving. As she was standing there against the light, I couldn't make out her face; her clothes formed a faint, colourful outline.

"My fine young man," she said in Turkish, "shall I tell your fortune?"

She was a Rom, a Turkish gypsy from the gypsy village of Kalkan-Dere. She came straight into the workshop. There she took on another form, another life. I could see her every detail: a shapely girl, copper-coloured and supple as a roe deer, dressed, like all the gypsies, in a multi-coloured flowery skirt, wide at the bottom with many ruffles, a velvet waistcoat, a yellow scarf on her head and a bright, scarlet flower behind her ear. She came slowly towards me swaying her hips. As she walked her long skirts raised a fine dust from the ground which surrounded her like a golden, glittering cloud.

I stopped work and gazed at her. I didn't understand what was happening inside of me. It was almost like a bright and joyful spring had entered our dark, gloomy workshop. She smiled, her eyes shone, her teeth whitely glistened and her lips became redder.

"My dark-eyed boy," she said as she neared me, "give me your hand and let me tell your fortune. The destiny of those eyes that will break so many hearts."

I offered my hand and gazed at her, now filled with longing. When I touched her hand, it seemed hot as fire.

"My eyes are black from the coal," I said.

"You're joking," she replied, gazing at me, "gold remains gold no matter how you dirty it."

She raised her leg, supporting it on a pile of cast iron, which allowed her shoulder bag to swing to the ground. Her skirts rustled like a deep breath coming from within her body.

"Be careful. You'll burn yourself," I said, and gathering together her lower skirts, I touched her bare leg.

"More than I'm burning already?" she said, looking me in the eye and taking hold of my naked arm.

At that moment she was very beautiful. I broke free from her grasp, grabbed her in my embrace and kissed her hard at the base of her neck, just above her hot chest.

"You'll knock me over, my tiger," she shouted, laughing and hugging, and kissed me.

"I'll have you over, come on!" I replied, and without letting her out of my embrace, like a predator holding tight to its prey, I carried her to the rear of the foundry where the unworked iron was piled up.

She didn't resist at all, only clung on to me and returned my wild kisses. Without speaking, we found ourselves on the packed, loose earth in the darkest part of the workshop. Outside the sun shone, and around us the dust raised by my heavy steps and her dragged skirts formed something like a curtain.

The Kalkan-Derelidisa whispered:

"My lion, you're what I've longed for," and kissed me passionately. I said nothing, simply moaned.

. . .

When we got up the dust had settled; the light was clear and I could see the marks I'd left all over her clothes and body, black marks from the smoke and fire.

"Look what I've done to you," I said sadly.

She caressed me with one hand and with the other wiped at the marks.

"Don't be upset my asikis. You're all over me as you are within me."

"And you're still there," I said laughing, pointing to the marks of her body outlined on the soft earth.

"You were worth it, my lover."

I embraced her again and began kissing her wherever my lips took me.

"My beauty, you're a levendissa, a derbederissa like all your race!"

She slipped smoothly out of my embrace, took me by the hand, "Come on let's go," and pulled me near to the doorway.

"Give me your left hand, the hand of the heart, so I can tell you your good destiny."

"My beauty," I replied, "what better fate could I have than what I've just enjoyed? I couldn't ask for more and it couldn't happen."

"Not only your eyes, but also your words break hearts," she replied and kissed me tenderly.

Once more she shook her skirts, which rustled joyfully, adjusted her scarf, and before I could embrace her again, she had skipped towards the doorway. She opened her arms wide in the arching rays.

"My tiger, I'll see you again."

And she was gone. I ran to follow her, but instead paused just beside the door to admire her. With one hand she'd taken hold of her scarf, while the other was on her hip forming a shape like the handle of a water jug, her head bent forward as she walked, hips swaying in the sunlight, with her shoulder bag swinging behind her as if caressing her hips.

When Master-Markos returned and went to hang his jacket at the back of the workshop he saw the marks on the ground.

"Hey Lanky," he shouted, that's what he called me. "What have you been up to this time?"

"It's nothing," I answered heavily.

I leaned over and picked up the gypsy's scarlet flower which had fallen, and with my foot slowly wiped away the marks on the ground.

The Kalkan-Derelidisa never appeared again...

THREE

The Dormitory of Bechlioul-Aga

At Galata, the commercial and naval centre of The City's port, near "Straight Street" where the tramway passed, sometimes pulled by two horses, at other times by four, were the popular hangouts: restaurants, cafes and wine houses, mixed up amongst large stores and smaller shops. There too, was the teahouse of Bechlioul-Aga. The Old Tea-Man had a double mission: in the daytime, winter and summer, he prepared tea and ran to serve it to his outside customers. At night the teahouse became a *sala*, a place for the homeless to sleep, known by the name "O Yatakhanes tou Bechlioul-Aga," that is to say, "The Dormitory of Bechlioul-Aga."

It was a large basement under a warehouse, down a narrow alley, deep as a ditch. At one end was an arched opening, wide and low, black like a gaping, toothless mouth, low on the muddy road. You entered down a worn stone-stairway, having to bend down, and after two or three paces you were swallowed up by the darkness of the basement: a long narrow space about fifteen metres long and roughly five metres wide.

On the low ceiling, blackened by smoke, you could just make out the beams; rough tree-trunks like huge warped veins. The unpainted walls, built of large rocks with dry mortar between them, formed a crudely made mosaic, as if for giants. Near the ceiling, thick cobwebs, black as clouds, half-covered the beams and the walls. Further down, the walls were mottled with dull tones of damp and dirt, some of which formed monstrous shapes. The lower walls—from the floor up to about the height of a man—were formed of round stones made smooth and shiny over the years by the backs of the dossers who had taken refuge and found uneasy rest at Bechlioul-Aga's shelter.

The black-earthed and damp ground absorbed both heavy footsteps and the din, and gave off the stench of mould; while the only source of light and air was the arched entranceway. The dim light and stifling air of the narrow alleyway entered the refuge through the mouth of that opening, which had no door and remained open night and day in the cold of winter and the heat of summer.

At the bottom of the stairs, which was close by to let a little light in, was the counter where Bechlioul-Aga prepared the tea. Arranged neatly on the counter were rows of Persian tea-glasses with their strange shapes, which resembled the tall, thin receptacles used by doctors for cupping blood. They were spotlessly clean and decorated with circular, golden lines; a luxury of the buried teahouse which only made more obvious its general bareness and squalor. The Old Tea-Man was proud of these glasses and looked after them like a treasure. At one end of the counter stood a large copper samovar which gleamed from the Old Tea-Man's rubbing. Scalding-hot water bubbled continuously inside it and steam rose like smoke from a censer. On top of the samovar, the rounded, blue porcelain teapot was enthroned, steaming with sweet-smelling Persian tea. At the other end was the wooden pail where the glasses were washed, and beside it a huge round jar, half-buried in the earth to keep the clean water cool.

Bechlioul-Aga was a Persian over seventy years old, clean, and with tidy habits, he spoke little, like all the decent, old men from the East. Religious and true to his prophet Ali, he had his hair and nails dyed with quinquina to ensure his entry into paradise when he died.

In the daytime, the aged Persian allowed no one to remain in his dormitory. He prepared tea and took it out to the surrounding shops. He slept very little, and during the quiet mid-afternoon hours, when there was little business, he would lay down beside his counter on a rough straw-mat, which he also used for his prayers, and slept lightly, ever ready to prepare a tea as soon as he heard the order. When evening came and the shops brought down their shutters, he finished his outside work; and as night fell and the alley became dark and empty the dormitory came to life.

Only then did the clients come. People of all sorts: all men—old, young, middle-aged, even children. Turks, Greeks, Armenians, Jews and others such as Arabs; all the races that made up the New Babylon that was Constantinople at the end of the nineteenth century. Sometimes, very rarely, there came some old female beggars. Most of these poor people were dressed in shabby, cast-off clothing: trousers ragged, jackets with a hundred patches, shirts—if they had one—and ripped. When someone had an overcoat, it was rough as an old sack. Some were shoeless, others dirty, many unshaven. But sometimes among them were one or two with more human clothing. The unfortunate children had nothing to cover themselves with, except rags tied with string, and were often shaking and cold. Amongst all these poor people, some had eaten a little and others had simply gone hungry.

They went down the basement stairs bent over, not speaking, silent, either one by one or sometimes two or three together. The talk, the arguing, the laughing, stopped at the entrance. Hounded from morning till night, they found a temporary home at Bechlioul-Aga's dormitory; there was no other refuge for them in the world but that of the Old Persian. As soon as they entered, they greeted him,

"Merhaba Baba"—the elderly in a whisper and the others more loudly, but all warmly—and each threw his small coin on the counter and ordered a tea, which he drank slowly, exchanging a few words with the old man.

A single lamp hanging from the centre of the ceiling struggled with its feeble light to penetrate the darkness, which was black as pitch. Along the two long-sides of the basement, on the ground, were rolled up sleeping mats of dry, rough straw, which looked like huge yellow and black snakes lurking at the base of the walls. The customers unrolled their mats, which were as wide as the body of a man, and spread them on the earthen floor along the two sides of the basement, leaving a narrow corridor down the middle.

Then each took his place on the spread-out mats which served as their beds. The loners were few; most gathered in small groups, all ages mixed together. Bechlioul-Aga knew most of them well, but only by nickname because no one used his real name. Others he remembered only vaguely, as the clientele was always changing. Often, for reasons of security, some left long gaps between their visits; who knows where they went and slept to hide their traces. Others, for the same reason, were newcomers. These newcomers, even if they had been brought by old customers, were watched carefully both by Bechlioul-Aga —whose motto was to deny shelter to no one—and by his regulars, so as to avoid any unforeseen trouble from someone who did not know the dormitory rules.

. . .

New and old customers of all ages loved Bechlioul-Aga and respected his simple discipline and tireless kindness, which awakened in their souls buried virtues. He was interested in their lives, and when they stumblingly told him of their troubles, the old man gave them courage with some proverb or with other words of comfort. All these persecuted people, with the Old Persian at their head, formed a patriarchal family which was constantly changing both in size and in make up.

Within that retreat, that chamber where the outcasts of society were crammed like cattle and slept like animals, no babel was heard, no quarrelling, no shouting. If occasionally, someone began to start a row, it was smothered before it could spread. An unwritten law, respected by all, ruled that every disagreement between these lost souls, even those that had to be settled by bloodshed, must be decided outside the holy asylum, either before they entered or after they left. Even when someone happened to come to the dormitory drunk, he obeyed the rules and kept quiet.

Bechlioul-Aga would have offered tea and a bed to all these wretched people for free, as an offering from his soul to his prophet Ali. But instead, the old man took for both tea and sleep one *besliki* (a five-cent coin) while for his daytime customers he charged one *metaliki* (two fivers). Thus, he gave these souls the satisfaction of paying only that five for tea and a bed, like free, worthy men, and not like the poor living on charity. It was different in the really cold weather, when he would offer two glasses of tea without counting the second one, and if someone was unable to pay, he gave it to them for nothing. In addition, by giving loans, many of which he did not expect to be returned, he found ways of helping others through their difficult times.

The Old Persian prepared tea for all that flock of poverty-stricken men with the same care that he took for his rich daytime customers. He preferred his *yavrumlar*, the younger customers, to remain close to him so he would have the pleasure of chatting with them and be sure that they got their drink; but whenever he was able, he brought the tea himself to the old, the disabled or those he especially respected. He presented it to them with a heartfelt, "May it bring you health." When he couldn't go himself, he sent one of the youngsters to take it to where one of his favourites was perched, so he could drink it comfortably while lounging in his corner. The youngsters took the rim-filled glasses slowly, being careful not to spill a drop of the beneficial hot drink that for many was the only thing on that day which would sweeten their wrung-out guts. Above all, they tried not to break any glass and distress the Old Aga, even though he never would have shown his true feelings. For this reason, they returned the glasses as soon as they were emptied and placed them on the counter, saying, "Thank you Old Father," so he could see they were undamaged.

A few of the customers arrived very late at night. These late comers drank their tea at the counter and then, silently, found whatever place they could among those already sleeping. An atmosphere of complete calm reigned in that chamber of the suffering, known and unknown to each other, innocent and guilty, kind and malicious. Under the dim light, some stretched-out all alone, to recollect who knows what actions or dreams. Others, in small groups, talked quietly, laid down plans and hoped for their success. That dive was not without its secret whisperings, pairings-off and hands playing over bodies. Each of these outcasts had his own "profession," one stranger than the other. All however, had only one aim: to secure their daily bread or leftovers, to scrape a living by stealing, fraud, or even with blood; because the others, the greedy ones, gave them no other means of survival and left them to die of hunger.

Slowly, these ravaged figures were overcome by sleep; deep and calm for some, for others, uneasy and distressing, causing their bodies, deprived of caresses, to lie in uniquely strange and contorted positions. In wintertime, when it was bitterly cold out in the alley and a killer wind brought in the freezing rain or scattered flakes of snow from the open doorway, these bodies became one living mass of warm matter, which pulsed, breathed and heaved noisily. One body could not be distinguished from the other, lying with limbs tightly entwined to keep warm.

Heads were lost between legs, arms around hips, bellies up against haunches, faces against chests, legs entwined with other legs, and hands rested wherever they found themselves. When it was really cold, the dogs from the street came into the dormitory seeking a little warmth and mixed in with the humans. Bechlioul-Aga was sorry for the freezing dogs and the customers accepted them like children—kind children—who loved and played with these good animals; all sleeping close together to keep warm.

In summer, the few vagrants who remained faithful to the Old Persian and their hangout preferred to sleep near the entrance to be cooled down by the polluted breath of dirty air that blew in from the alleyway. In winter, however, when the dormitory was mostly full with the homeless, they all crowded together in the depths of the basement as far away from the door as possible. When it was biting cold, with snow and frost outside, they lit a small fire at the rear of the den, using wood they had stolen from nearby shops or from fences and houses further away. Even though Bechlioul-Aga didn't approve of this—as there was always a danger of fire in that Great Capital where most of the houses were built of wood—in frosty weather he accepted it, so his "Children of Allah," as he called them, could warm their frozen bones and shivering flesh for a while. He kept a wary eye on them though and made sure they were careful.

Everyone gathered around that beneficial fire. Those who were nearest sat cross-legged on the ground in a circle and fed it with wood, poking at it to form embers and to make it last longer and extend its warmth as long as possible. Behind them, a second circle formed of those who squatted or knelt. The last and biggest group stood upright, packed tightly together with one against the other. In order to warm their hands and arms, they held them forwards and over the heads and backs of those in front; and after they had warmed a bit, thrust them against their frozen chests and rubbed their faces, which were blue with cold. As if from some residue of inherent humanity, like dancers changing places in a dance, when they had warmed up, those nearest the fire moved back and gave their places to others from further behind, until, drowsy from the heat and the joy of the fire, they all allowed it to go out and lay down to sleep.

All night, under the dull light of the lamp, those packed bodies enjoyed the only rest they could find in all of their deprived lives. Only Bechlioul-Aga remained awake, and with his compassionate eyes kept watch over the suffering pack of humans who found rest under his roof.

However, even that sleep was not without danger. To show their zeal, the police carried out surprise raids on the dormitory and ruined the outcasts' rest. Their situation then became tragic as all were overcome with fear that they would be thrown into prison cells. Then Bechlioul-Aga, the *merhametli*, the kind-hearted one, would intervene and attempt to persuade the upholders of order —who were taught by their masters to care nothing for human misfortune—to act as The Prophet did and not disturb the holy sleep of these poor people, but to sort things out early in the morning when they woke up. He guaranteed their presence and placed himself at the disposal of the police. Sometimes he succeeded in gaining a temporary delay, sometimes not. Those who were taken out with shoves and curses and taken to the police station were filled with bitterness. The hearts of those who remained behind were beating hard with joy at their escape, and with anxiety about the fate of their friends, a fate which no one could know once they had been snatched by the law.

As soon as the dawn broke sweetly, the night's strugglers awoke and were ready to leave; the wariness which had become an unwritten law forbade them to stay in the basement after first light. Those who had a few coins in their pockets drank a morning tea to get their circulation going. The others would have left without even one sip if not for the old man, who treated them to a morning glass. Before they left, each one had to roll-up his straw-mat and place it at the foot of the wall, exactly as he had found it. If it happened that someone was still sleeping heavily, they woke him up with a friendly kick in the arse. Stooping and silent, as they had entered, they came out of that dark den into the dawn light of an uncertain day, to renew the same hard and impoverished life. Only the children were allowed to sleep longer, and when they awoke the Old

Persian gave them each a glass of tea and a simit, and always slipped one or two copper coins into their pockets.

May your days be happy, if you still live. May your soul be hallowed if you have died, Bechlioul-Aga, the kind-hearted one. During the harshest and most difficult days of my life I found refuge in your dormitory.

FOUR

The Butcher's Shop of Petro-Kalfa

I was about fifteen when I went as an apprentice to the butcher's shop of my cousin Petro-Kalfa. I stayed there for less than a year, but I learned quite a few things. The shop was at Pera, the great European quarter of the city, at a central position opposite the Aga Djami mosque. It had quite a large clientele and did good business. My cousin, without being a genuine butcher, did alright with this work because he was skilful and could do well at whatever he turned his hand to, as long as he had the desire.

He had tried his hand at many professions and had learnt carpentry; however, above all, he liked to design and build houses. That's why they called him "Petro-Kalfa" or "Master Builder," though at the time he was a butcher. He loved horses, having a good time, and women; and on these he spent all the money which passed through his hands, both his own and that of others. He liked me because I was a little like him, open-handed and unruly. He had more faith in me than in his partner, an Albanian, who was a specialist in slaughtering and in meat-cuts.

My cousin, occupied as he was with horses and women, didn't spend a lot of time in the shop; however, he kept an open eye on business. One day he said to me:

"Stavri, when you see the meat changing colour and darkening or growing hard, cut some very thin slices off, like shavings, so that it looks red and fresh. If you like, cook the offcuts and eat them, or if you prefer, give them to the poor."

In those days there were no refrigerators, or even ice-blocks, only snow that was kept in pits; and that was only used in exceptional circumstances. The meat was kept fresh in air-currents. The butcher's shop must never face the sun and be as open as possible on all sides. It must never be closed at night by solid doors, but only railed-in, so the cool draughts of air can enter from all sides. But these methods, although they preserved the meat, dried it out and caused it to darken.

So, given the idea by my cousin, along with my other tasks, I began a new one. Instead of eating the offcuts myself, I prepared them as a meze and invited the boss and his partner to join me. Both of them thought this a good idea and from then on it was one of my jobs to prepare the meze; now and then giving some of it to the poor. So, almost every day, there was at the shop some "Kebab a la Hasap," sometimes souvlakia and sometimes "djizbiz," that is köfte on the grill. It seems I managed the art of cooking well, as my two bosses relished the meze and longed for more.

Among the butcher's customers was a wine merchant who had a huge storehouse with many kinds of wine. As well as buying meat for his home, he took all the blood from the slaughtered animals to mix with his new wine and sometimes even with the older reds. He said that the blood cleansed the wine and gave it a fine smell and taste. I had the thought that, as he was a customer, we could have some good wine with our meze, and I started to order wine from him to accompany our little snacks; I chose the best Pasalimani. The same thing happened with a customer who was a baker, he supplied me with small loaves that were fresh and hot.

Petro-Kalfa and the Albanian were very pleased with these evening snacks, eaten before their main meal, and slowly they became real feasts. I made sure they happened regularly even when the meat had not blackened, because with the constant shaving it always looked fresh. That's what my cousin and boss wanted, and he was doubly pleased with his "adopted son" for keeping the meat fresh and making good use of the offcuts; so pleased, in fact, that he began bringing his friends to stuff themselves. For my troubles, I was given a generous share, and I constantly heard "Aferim Stavri! — Bravo Stavri!" from the boss and his guests.

. . .

Unfortunately, this revelry didn't last long. The moment came when both the boss and the Albanian realised that more meat was "blackening" than was being sold. At the same time, when we sent our accounts to the wine merchant and the baker for the meat we supplied to their homes, they responded with their own bills, which amounted to just as much; in fact, the wine merchant's was more.

"Hey Stavri," said my cousin, the boss, "we've become the best customers of our own butcher's shop. A lot of meat must have gone black!"

"Well," I replied, "didn't you tell me to shave the black from the meat so it would always look red and fresh? That's what I did, and with the offcuts I made meze, which you and your friends thought were wonderful, together with the wine and fresh loaves, and you kept congratulating me. What do you want to happen now?"

"Yes, Stavri, what you say is true. But we must find another way to manage things."

And we found a way.

With the shavings and other meat that was left over, we made *soutzoukakia*. But they were so tasty we ate them as snacks for more feasts, and it became a habit. So, the partying continued as before, only now we drank rakı, which went down better with the *soutzoukakia*. Again, we became the best customers of our own shop, the number of guests multiplied, and the fame of butcher Petro-Kalfa spread.

In the meantime, the hour had come when my restless

boss became bored with being a butcher and set his course for a new profession and new adventures. By then the suppliers had had enough, and on the other hand, my cousin was spending freely on the horses and his women. He changed between them so often that one day I said to him, "Sometime when you're drunk, Boss, you'll get mixed up and take some girlfriend for a horse and some mare for a woman." He laughed unconcernedly.

The creditors came and went more frequently, but Petro-Kalfa did the opposite; he was often absent and didn't appear for days. His partner, the Albanian, faced the problem alone, as the shop was in his name. That was Petros's way, a jack-of-all-trades and a useless businessman with other peoples' money. However, he wasn't a fraudster or a blackmailer; when things didn't go well, he simply stepped aside. Despite that, nobody held a grudge against him because, underneath it all, he was good-hearted. He was so good-hearted, open-handed and fond of partying, that people forgave him, and they always remained friends; saying with a smile, "It's the will of Allah."

Over time it had become his easygoing habit to change professions and partners as often as he changed horses and women. However, before he abandoned one business, he devised the next one and got it up and running in a flash. With his smooth-talking and easy ways, he always found some backer to believe in him. When the butcher's shop started to worry him, he arranged to take on a contract to restore a large house on the opposite side of the city, along with a marble mason he knew. It had always been his ambition to be a builder, as this was the craft that interested him above all others, his passion, and every now and again he returned to it. All the other jobs he did in between were side hustles which gave variety to his ever-changing life.

For a while he disappeared. Then he came back, and with the help of the Albanian managed to sell some things, come to a deal with the creditors and close the shop; saying, in his turn, "It's the will of Allah."

So came to an end the fun with the kebabs, the *soutzoukakia*, the red wine, the rakı and the little loaves that were fresh and hot.

FIVE

Pokris & Siranush: Overpowering Love

At Mastro-Pandias's foundry the master-craftsman was "Pokris o Pivatianos," lithe and strongly built. His ruggedly handsome face was sweetened by his chestnut eyes, abundant blond hair and a thick moustache. A fine young fellow who, if he had wished to, could have broken many hearts, but he was absorbed in his work and wounded by a secret love.

As a caster of iron, he was one of the best, and he knew some letters as he had attended a junior school at Selimpaşa (Epivates), the large Greek village in Thrace, on the Sea of Marmara. He had learnt his craft from one of the most famous iron-casters in The City, the Armenian "Artin Usta," whose work was considered exceptional by the English who were responsible for running the Sultan's Naval Yards.

He had taught Pokris to throw a special dust, the composition of which was a secret, into the molten metal while it was still boiling. Faced by the fire and molten metal he became another person, all strength and lissomness; you'd think he was on fire too as his body swayed along with the flames, and like a magician, he shaped the metal into whatever form he wished. As he poured the molten metal into the mould, he watched it so closely that he was in danger of burning his face and scorching his open chest and bare arms. A little closer and he would have plunged his hands into that consuming fire, taken handfuls of the metal, and rubbed it between his fingers to test its quality. At various times during the heating he would pour off a little into moulds the size of soap bars. He made some patterns on them and when they had cooled, he began his trials; shaping them, breaking them, pounding them, all attention and thought.

From the moment he started work, early in the morning before all the others, until the time he finished, last of all, he didn't stop except to have a snack. As I was younger than he was, I admired and took pride in him. It was a joy to watch him working, and it might have been the way he went about his work that caused me to love the craft back then. Mastro-Pandias, the boss, respected and listened to him because he made money from his efforts. He kept Pokris happy in any way he could so that he would stay at the foundry and so it wouldn't lose the reputation he had brought to it. Pokris, honest craftsman that he was, respected Pandias and dedicated himself to his work.

When that strong worker, that transformer of metals,

that handsome man, took off his leather work-apron you'd say he'd also removed his manliness and all its glow. When he put on his street clothes, he seemed to dress himself in bitterness and worry. His bearing slumped, his movements became heavy and his words few, as if he was going to a funeral. Only his eyes shone deeply, mirroring the yearning that tormented him. He would mutter a dry "Yeia sas — Goodbye everyone," and leave. He had no family in The City; his mother and a married sister lived at Epivates. He rarely went to a tavern with others, but usually withdrew to some small café where he sat alone reading a newspaper and drinking his coffee.

I was fond of him and wanted his company, but our habits were very different; he was quiet, serious, a loner, while I was boiling with a thirst for life and got mixed up in everything.

The reason for his thoughtfulness and bitterness was love. Pokris was in love with a "public woman," an inmate of a *kerhane*, a brothel in Çiçek Sokak (Flower Street), who was an Armenian named Siranush, tall and beautiful like him, but dark-complexioned with black hair, playful eyes and a well-formed body. Siranush loved Pokris deeply, and came now and then to see him at the foundry; always at the midday hours when there was no business at the bordello and our workshop was quiet, since the craftsmen and apprentices had gone out to eat and drink their coffee.

The two of them withdrew to a dark place at the rear

of the foundry and sat near each other on piles of unworked iron. Pokris with his leather apron doubled on his lap and his jacket thrown over his shoulders, his face red from the fire and blackened by smoke, and Siranush dressed simply and neatly like a young married woman. They held hands and gazed into each other's eyes, silent and unmoving. Occasionally exchanging a few words, they sighed frequently and sometimes their eyes filled with tears as though a great evil lay heavy upon them.

At first I didn't realise what she did, but I came across her one night in the Çiçek Sokak in a gaudy dress she worked in and recognised her, much as she tried to avoid me. The next day, I casually teased Pokris about his girlfriend the "goody-goody," as I called her. He didn't get angry, just looked at me with a glance both fearful and imploring and said, "Stavri, my boy, don't bother her." I was flattered, thinking he was afraid I'd take her away from him, and said nonchalantly, "What do I want from whores? I can look after my youth and my money."

He grabbed my arm, looked at me for a while strangely, and avoiding my eyes, muttered quietly, "Thanks, Stavri," and then added, as if talking to himself, "Siranush isn't that type." And in truth Siranush was a woman worthy of respect, as I realised when I got to know her better. That's why I loved her as I loved Pokris, and I watched over their lives as if they were members of my own family. When they met at the foundry, I didn't allow any of the lads to enter until Siranush had left. Sometimes I felt sorry for them when I saw how melancholy they were, and said laughing, "Come on you two, do you just gaze at each other like idiots? Go on, kiss. I won't look," and I turned my back on them.

Then I heard deep sighs and a timid noise which would have been their kiss. Although I avoided speaking to Pokris about their love, I was aware that his behaviour towards me was becoming more intimate, as if he had faith in me. Certainly Siranush would have told him how I behaved to her when I happened to visit the bordello where she worked. We greeted each other like old friends, without the words and flirting that were usual in that environment; and so Pokris began to tell me details about their story.

One day when Siranush was at the workshop, I saw her rolling some of Pokris's clothes into a bundle to take home with her. This made an impression on me; I stared at Pokris as, with a tender glance, he watched her leaving. He understood my puzzlement, turned to me and said, "You see it's impossible for me to persuade her not to wash my clothes, though I've begged her not to. Do you know what she answered? 'Let me do it Pokri, when I'm washing your clothes I feel as if I'm rinsing clean the dirtiness of my life,'" and tears came into his eyes.

I was moved too. "Well, Pokri," I said, "I love her too. She's a wonderful being."

Along with his other habits Pokris ate very little. I couldn't understand how, after such tiring work, his strong body could make do with so little food. He wasn't a miser;

so why did he eat so little? Maybe he was ill? One day I laid on a spread there at the workshop.

"Eat up Pokri!" I shouted at him. "You'll get sick the way you're going on, what with your love and the way you're not eating."

"I'll eat well," he answered, "in my own house when my wife, Siranush, is cooking for me."

He told me confidentially that the two of them were saving money so they could pay off the *kerhanedzou* (the madam), and buy Siranush's freedom, and also for him to build a house for them to live in when they married. This moved me so much that I came to look on them as my brother and sister whom I had to help to get their lives back in order. Then, another incident made my feelings for them become sacred.

I knew that from time to time Pokris went to the brothel to meet Siranush and spend the whole night with her. One day I suggested to him that we go together to the festival at Kalpha, famous for the dionysiac parties of the gypsies who took part. But he took it as if I had committed some sin or crime.

"Ah, no!" he shouted, "no Stavri, not to such a place without my wife Siranush."

"Forget it then," I said, a little angry myself, "to hell with it! Are you afraid you'll pick up gonorrhoea there and pass it on to Siranush one of the nights you spend with her?"

Pokris suddenly turned and stared at me, his eyes wide and angry. He had gone pale, his jaw was clenched and he was panting, "What are you saying?!" He shouted threateningly, grabbing my arm, "me and Siranush...the nights we spend together...gonorrhoea...don't say that again Stavri!"

And, as if he couldn't think or speak, and wanted to prevent himself from suffering, or doing any harm, he squeezed my arms hard. I felt sorry for him from the bottom of my heart. I hadn't realised the depth of their love.

"What's wrong with you Pokri?" I said in a voice full of sympathy and regret, removing his hands from my arms and holding them in mine.

"Forgive me," I added humbly, looking him in the eyes, "what a love that is of yours!"

"Stavri, my brother," he replied, "you should know how we suffer..." and his lips trembled.

We sat down on a pile of iron and after a short silence he told me the story of their love from the beginning.

He met Siranush for the first time at the same brothel he had been visiting for two years. He took a liking to her and from then on always went with her. He found in her something the other public women lacked. Something like affection, a sweet homeliness. One time he told her this and even added that he thought she was cut out to be a mother. Siranush grabbed his hands and with tears in her eyes said, "Dear man, nobody's ever said anything like that to me." And she kissed him. From then on he saw her more regularly and one night she told him her story, almost as if she was confessing and asking for forgiveness.

She was an orphan, and some distant relatives who kept her as a sort of neglected child put her to work in an Armenian's scarf factory. There she was seduced by the boss's son, who promised to marry her even if the two of them had to run away to the end of the world. But when the youth confessed to his father that he loved Siranush and wished to marry her, the old man threw her out of the factory and threatened to disinherit his precious son. The youth was terrified and abandoned Siranush. Alone and in despair, she left Kondoskali where she worked and set off for the unknown Great City. Crossing the Bridge of Galata in the dark, she went to throw herself into the sea. But she was prevented from jumping by a passer-by, who supposedly wished to save her, but had other plans which he immediately tried to put into effect. Terrified, she broke free from his grasp and ran off. She spent the night walking, seeking refuge, like a hunted animal, in the dark corners of whatever street opened up before her. She passed, fearfully, through some well-lit places full of people, then descended steep slopes where the earth and stones slipped under her feet and brought her to her knees two or three times. Finally, exhausted and weak with hunger, she laid down at the foot of a wall inside a building site and slept till dawn.

She was woken by something warm passing over her face and hair. She opened her eyes, too exhausted to be frightened. It was day, and she saw an old lady in black bent over her and regarding her with sympathy. The woman caressed her and whispered some words like a lullaby which she didn't understand. Slowly, though her head and body were still aching, she felt pleasure from the words and from the cool morning breeze, which brought with it the faint sound of a *laterna*, playing a soulful tune. The old lady grasped her under the armpits and helped her to her feet, softly speaking some Turkish words that warmed her heart. She walked while supported by the woman, who was now talking to her of a new life full of joys and happiness. As they proceeded, the sound of the *laterna* grew louder and more pleasing. After a while, they entered a narrow lane with low houses painted in bright colours which glowed in the clear morning light. Cheerful voices, laughter and song were coming from one of the buildings, along with the sound of the *laterna*, and Siranush felt as if she was walking through a dream. The old lady pushed open a door and they entered one of the houses. A second, lower door led them into a small, warm room which smelled of food, coffee and lavender. Siranush, as if enlivened by the warmth and pleasant smells, opened her eyes wide and looked all around her. A chubby, gaudily dressed woman sat before a brazier smoking and preparing coffee. She raised her eyes and looked from Siranush to the old lady in surprise. The latter, with a quick movement of her small eyes filled her in. Whereupon the fat woman rose heavily to her feet, took Siranush by the hand and welcomed her with joy and kindness, as if she were some relative she'd been expecting for a long time, and sat her down snugly on the soft, low divan. Siranush hesitantly let this kind woman do as she wished. My God, what a good reception it was in that warm little room. How many times had she longed for such a cozy corner of her own. The warmth of the brazier brought relief to her aching body, the smells spoke to her of easy living, and these two good women couldn't do enough for her, letting her eat, drink, even smoke—something she had never done before, but which she tried and liked. Nobody had ever treated her like that. How she longed to stay there. And that's what happened.

Sad, lonely and despairing, she gradually agreed to all that the cunning, fat woman asked her to do, while the old lady calmed her down with her cajolery whenever she complained or made a fuss. She no longer had the strength to really understand what was happening to her or to resist. It was as if the youthful Siranush had died along with her betrayed love. And so she began the new life of a woman who, unwillingly, sold her body and false love to the customers of that small brothel at Bülbül Dere—without having enjoyed the true, youthful love that her whole being thirsted for. In a short while, thanks to her beauty, she had driven crazy two or three wealthy customers who helped her rise up the hierarchy of prostitution to end up at the *kibariko*—the "respectable" bordello of Kior-Eliza in the Çiçek Sokak in Pera. There she continued her melancholy life, which as time passed, she found empty, joyless and bitter.

Pokris, a mature man by now, had never got seriously involved with a woman as he had never fallen in love; nor had he got engaged, despite the many proposals made to him by intermediaries. He felt for Siranush with all the love he held within his pure heart, and she loved him, despairingly, with all her orphaned soul. Together they began to make plans: to build a small house, to free Siranush from the bonds of prostitution, to marry. From the day they made that decision, every night they spent together was a chastening ordeal. Until morning they sat side by side, hand in hand, looking into each other's eyes—sometimes bemoaning their fate, sometimes planning their future, sometimes remaining silent. On no night did they lie together, but sat instead like two innocent and virgin children.

On the same street as our workshop were other foundries. For that reason it was called "Ta Dokmetzidika" or "Street of the Foundries." One of them had formerly belonged to the late, famed *dokmetzis* Artin Usta, and had been taken over by one of his co-religionists. A former pupil of Artin's worked there, another Armenian master-craftsman called Dikran. He was about twenty-eight years old, strongly built with regular features, black eyes and a moustache which he shaped like that of the Kaiser. His hair was curly and he oiled it with pomade so that it shone greasily. Although he looked a fine young fellow, he was unlikeable as he played the "tough guy" in a conceited and heavy-handed way. He interfered in everyone's affairs and boasted that all other *dokmetzides* were worthless compared to him and that he was an even better craftsman than the late Artin Usta. I'd been out drinking with him a few times in the past, but we had nothing in common and I avoided him. He didn't care much for me and was itching to find some reason to create trouble with my companions and our workshop, and he did. One day he spotted Siranush coming out of our foundry. He followed her and when he saw that she was a shapely girl he spoke to her provocatively in the style of a lady-killer. Without stopping, she turned her head, looked him in the eye and boldly told him to "Get lost!" He replied with an indecent gesture and coarse language. Siranush stopped abruptly, turned to face him and shouted angrily, "Aren't you ashamed, big man, to behave so improperly to a woman?" and continued on her way. He didn't follow her, but swore and threatened her, "You won't escape me because, just like all women, you're good for nothing but bed!"

From then on he kept an eye on our place; who went in, who came out. Like the tough guy he thought he was, he didn't consider it proper to carry out the task himself, but put a young Turkish apprentice of his, Nedjip, to keep him informed. Siranush told Pokris about the incident and he, suspecting Dikran's intentions, told her to be cautious. From then on she came and went at irregular hours so as not to be spotted and to avoid coming face to face with Dikran, who was infuriated by the contempt she had shown him.

One evening I was out drinking with a group of acquaintances, Dikran among them. After a while the conversation came round to dealings with women and Dikran boasted that Siranush was his "secret conquest." I was a little drunk and said thoughtlessly, "Come on! What 'secret conquest'? Everyone knows she's a prostitute." Dikran immediately wanted to know which brothel she worked in, but as much as he insisted I refused to tell him. Quite a while after that, the same group of us were drinking again. When it grew late Dikran suggested continuing the party in some red-light house and I—again thoughtlessly—suggested going to the bordello of Kior-Eliza in the Çiçek Sokak. I had a reason to suggest it as I fancied a girl who worked there; a blonde, blue-eyed Romanian, fresh as warm bread, who played waltzes, allegras and fine *karsilamades* on the piano.

That brothel stood out from the others because the madam, Kior-Eliza, a *lecha*, a German-Jewish woman from Poland, had decorated the place in European style. The reception room had armchairs and curtains of cherry-coloured velvet, a piano and a phonograph, and she didn't allow any barrel-organs inside. The shade around the red light at the door had holes in it which formed the shapes of naked women. The beds in the rooms had tulle curtains around them, like those of a bride, while green, blue and rose-coloured candles were scattered here and there. Instead of bowls to wash in, there were "*bidets-ala-franga*" or "*binedes*" as the Turkish girls called them. When we had made ourselves comfortable in the salon and they had brought us the drinks and mezes we had ordered, the girls began to enter. Siranush was among them and she didn't notice that Dikran was with us. However, he immediately approached her and began to speak provocatively. At first she paid little attention, but he became more aggressive and lewd. It was clear he wanted to humiliate her and I realised the mistake I'd made bringing him to that house. I froze. It was as if I'd betrayed Pokris. I began thinking how I could get us out of there fast and forestall the trouble I feared was about to break out. Siranush threw an angry glance at me as if to scold me for what I'd done. Attempting to fix things and change the course they seemed to be taking, I said to Dikran softly, "*Azizim*, what's all this carrying on? You're shaming us in front of these good-hearted girls who are our friends. The way you're talking to that girl is upsetting them and is an insult to all of us," and turning to Siranush, I added, "don't take it badly girl, he's just excited; he's drunk too much. Anyway, we won't stay here all night. We'll just enjoy ourselves here for a little while longer and then we'll leave."

But Siranush didn't hold back: "Aren't you ashamed?"

she said to me with controlled rage. "You, a decent young guy going out with such a *külhanbeyi*—a hooligan!"

Before she could finish, Dikran shouted threateningly, "You go where the hell you want! I'm staying here to party as long as I like with this *kaltak*—this whore." He grabbed Siranush by the waist and breasts and tried to sit her on his lap, adding commandingly, "Right here. In front of you all..."

But Siranush, with a strong shove of both her hands against his face and chest, managed to break free and ran towards the door. Dikran, reacting fast, snatched at the wide sleeve of her robe, which tore off and remained in his left hand, while with his right he moved to draw his pistol from his rear trouser pocket.

The other girls were terrified and ran screaming to hide in the corners of the room and behind the furniture. Two of us jumped on Dikran and grabbed his arms to restrain him, while I, trying to calm the girls, shouted at him, "Dikran, are you crazy? Do you want to get us all into trouble?"

He struggled like a maniac to break free, shouting incoherently. Siranush stopped short, turned, and looking at him with eyes like daggers, shouted as if nailing him with her words, "Useless bully...and you an Armenian!" And went out the door, slamming it behind her.

At that moment, from another door, Kior-Eliza entered with a couple more of her girls and a pimp, whose whole manner said "Stand aside, I'm here." The Madam made out she was wild with rage, though she seemed to be shitting herself as if a murder had taken place. She didn't give a damn about anyone's blood being spilt but was worried about her furniture. Kior-Eliza was a woman of about fifty, flabby-faced, with blotchy hair, like European pickles, from the many times she had dyed it in an attempt to look younger. One of her eyes was smaller than the other, with the lower lid swollen, heavy and half-open. But the pupil shone like coals, you'd say she saw better out of that eye than with the other—the regular one, which shone like marble. It was because of those ill-matched eyes that they called her Kior-Eliza, or Blind Eliza.

"That useless woman's always making trouble for me," she shouted, "upsetting and abusing respectable clients." She turned to Dikran and stroked his hair, "Don't let it spoil your fun my fine young fellow. I've got other sweet-talking girls, as cool as water, who will make your bird sing. Not that mare! I'll show the no-good Armenian, with the lady-like airs she puts on ever since she fell in love with that stinking Greek. She'll pay dearly. I won't let her get my beautiful lokal closed down."

Dikran had been struggling like a lunatic to escape our grasp and threatening to slaughter and burn. When he heard Kior-Eliza's last words he made a tremendous final effort and burst free.

"What did you say?" he roared, "She's an Armenian?!"

"Yes," Kior-Eliza answered indifferently, "and her name is Siranush."

"Ach, what a bitch," growled Dikran, and turning to us,

"let's go," he said like an order and added through gritted teeth, "she won't escape me the whore."

Although we'd have preferred to stay, we took hold of him, two on each arm, and headed for the exit. The girls saw that they couldn't keep us there, despite their entreaties and wiles and began bitterly cursing Siranush and Dikran, who had spoiled the fun and the evening. But when we had gone down the stairs and were about to open the front door to leave, they all gathered on the landing above and shouted down to us, laughing, "We'll make it up to each other another time."

From then on things got worse and took an ugly turn, and against my will, I got involved; which was partly my own fault. Dikran was spiteful since he hadn't made Siranush his, and even more so because she loved Pokris, whom he had disliked for a long time. He was jealous of him because all the metalworkers recognised him, and not Dikran, as the best of all the late Artin Usta's former apprentices. Pokris's boss, even though he was an Armenian, said of the Greek that no other ironworker could compare with him. After his failure with Siranush, Dikran hated Pokris with all the fanaticism of a heretic Armenian for an Orthodox Greek. He tried in every way he could, no matter how underhanded and dishonourable, to get his hands on Siranush and humiliate her. But she stood like an unshakeable column before all his attacks. Neither the grumblings of Kior-Eliza nor the remarks of the other girls nor Dikran's threats could frighten her or make her change her mind.

One evening Dikran and two Turkish friends got drunk together and then went around to Kior-Eliza's place at a time when there were plenty of comings and goings. Siranush locked herself in her room as soon as she saw them, and they tried to break open the door. They had gone there with the intention of running off with her, threatening, with pistols and knives in their hands, that they would smash the place up. Kior-Eliza, although pissing herself with fright, managed to inform some contacts she had at the main police station at Galatasaray what was going on. They quickly arrived in force, surrounded the *lokal*, nabbed the three tough-guys and started to cart them off to the nick. But when Kior-Eliza saw that the big trouble had been forestalled, she begged the policemen, who were free customers of her place, to let the three go. So they released Dikran and his two friends, threatening that if they caused any more trouble at that "quiet house" they would face not only prison, but possible exile from the city.

When Dikran saw that method had failed, he thought up other schemes. One day, he sent an Armenian priest whom he had paid well, round to the brothel to threaten Siranush with the wrath of God and the Church for her great sin of falling in love with a Greek. The priest told her that if she married Pokris, she would go to hell, where devils would torment her for all eternity with fire and other tortures, each one more terrible than the last. Siranush listened to him patiently and at one point, when he had paused for breath, asked, "My priest, how is it a sin that I don't lie with the Greek until we are married, but it isn't a sin that all the other races of the world pass over my body every day?"

He said that wasn't a sin because it was her job and all work was honourable; but that marrying a Greek would be renouncing her faith, an unforgivable sin, and she would go straight to hell.

"Listen Mr Priest," she replied decisively, "there can't be a worse hell than the one I live in and yours doesn't scare me. Don't waste your words. When I marry the man who loves me, and whom I worship, I'll be saved from this hell here."

Then the priest opened the bundle he had with him and took out the vestments they wear when administering communion to someone who is about to die. He lit a black candle like those they place beside the dead, raised his arms high above his head and with all the fanaticism and malice he could muster excommunicated Siranush for the sin she was about to commit. She regarded him as if she was watching a Karagöz puppet theatre. When he had finished and repacked his bundle, she offered him a glass of cognac, saying with a smile, "Well my little priest, drink that for your trouble. But you've wasted your efforts and the money of whoever sent you."

The priest drank the cognac with one gulp and left running, as if Beelzebub himself was after him.

Things became even more difficult for the two lovers and they very rarely managed to see each other. Kior-Eliza wouldn't let Siranush out and the latter had made Pokris swear not to come to the brothel as she feared Dikran's reaction. On his part, Pokris was fearful for Siranush's life, isolated as she was, and was desperate to see her. He had become a nervous wreck. He came and went as though harassed and barely spoke. Sometimes he worked like a maniac, at others he stopped and fell into a reverie. He grew thin as he neither ate nor drank and his skin became black and yellow like Saint John the Beggar's.

One time, Siranush managed to come to the workshop at a late hour. She entered through the back door, dressed almost like a beggar-woman. To see them for the little time they were together would have made your heart weep. Another time, she sent a message to Pokris and met him at the bordello at Bülbül Dere where she had first fallen low and where the patrona still loved her. The next day when he entered the workshop, I thought I was seeing a corpse risen from its coffin. I went to speak to him, but he stopped me with an abrupt movement. He began working, but neither his eyes nor his mind was on his work, and at the end of the day he left like a hunted man, without saying a word. I was deeply sorry for him and felt I should do something to help him and Siranush but couldn't think of any solution. I just kept an eye out that Dikran didn't do him any underhanded harm. The Armenian was becoming more and more infuriated by his failures and tightened his apprentices' watch over our place in the hope of taking revenge at an unexpected moment. His reputation as a "tough guy" was in danger of becoming ridiculous, as he was vain and a windbag. He boasted that he had us all terrified and would soon "sort us out." All the workshops in the street waited with interest to see how this whole affair would end.

One evening I bought a drink for Nedjip, the young apprentice Dikran was training to be a tough guy. I tried to find out from him what Dikran was planning. Nedjip was a likeable, crazy kid who wanted my company and was pleased we were drinking together. He led me to understand, without actually saying so, that his boss was waiting for the right opportunity, which supposedly his machinations would bring about, and then take revenge on both Pokris and Siranush.

"And you, what will you do?" I asked him suddenly in a friendly way, looking him straight in the eyes.

He regarded me boldly and answered smiling, "Me? Nothing, I'm not crazy enough to get involved in trouble. I'll keep out of it."

"Bravo Nedjip!" I said, slapping him on the back. "You're an honest lad. That's the way!"

"What do you expect me to do?" he continued, "He's the master-craftsman and I'm the apprentice. He's got me in his hands and can do what he likes with me. I've got to keep on good terms with him, so I pretend to obey. To hell with him, let him believe I'm devoted to him..."

. . .

In the meantime, Dikran resorted to another underhanded method—the worst—the most dishonourable for a man. He made out that he'd fallen in love with Kior-Eliza. She liked him because he was a fine, strong young fellow while she was like an over-ripe pear, and she anointed him her "protector." Siranush had been saving ever since she and Pokris had decided to marry. She limited her spending on makeup, toiletries and trinkets, only buying what was necessary for her profession. The more devoted she became to her love for Pokris and their dreams for the future, the more she neglected herself and her work; something which was noticed by the customers who came to the bordello specially to visit her. Among them were two or three rich men smitten by her beauty. When they heard the details of her story, they offered to pay off her debt and set her up in a "house," and then she could marry whoever she wished. But Siranush refused, saying she'd rather be a free bird in the cage of the *kerhane* than "Madam of the House."

Dikran opened Kior-Eliza's eyes to this suspicious situation, saying that the way Siranush was letting herself go and neglecting her work was costing Kior-Eliza the money she was owed and pushed her to demand to be paid. He also got her to buy toiletries on Siranush's account so she'd attract more customers, whether she wanted to or not.

Siranush realised that she had reached a dead-end and

wouldn't be able to pay her debt and obtain her freedom. She would be condemned to this miserable life forever. If she left without paying, she could end up in prison. If she refused to pay and went to court, she wouldn't win, because even though these debts weren't recognised by law, they were silently accepted as essential and natural for professions of that type. In such cases no prostitute could win no matter how many lovers she had interested in her case. She was alone, while the Madam of the brothel had a whole battalion of supporters; the friends and lovers of the other inmates of the bordello, many of whom held positions in society or the state. She had them in her hands since she knew what each of them desired and paid them with alluring flesh. She also employed another tactic, obliging each of her girls to have a policeman as "protector." As for the other girls—although kind and distressed—they couldn't help Siranush as they were trapped in the Madam's snare. The life of an inmate in a bordello was in the hands of the patrona, just as in the years of slavery the life of a slave was in the hands of his master.

Caught up in this situation, with all its dangers, Pokris and Siranush resembled two incurably ill people; he was a wreck. They decided to abandon the idea of building a small home and to put together all the money they had saved and pay-off Siranush's debt. But the sum demanded by Kior-Eliza, encouraged by Dikran, was more than twice the amount they had saved. How could they do it? How could they find the money? I suffered too as I felt sorry for them but couldn't think of a way to help them escape from the nightmare. Like a woman, I could only encourage them and give them words of sympathy. I hadn't saved even one franc to give them and didn't have anything valuable to sell. Mastro-Pandias lent them a sum, but they still couldn't meet the amount demanded by Kior-Eliza. Nor would she agree to let them pay her off in instalments, even guaranteed by Mastro-Pandias.

One day at the foundry, Pokris was different; he seemed to have lost his reason. He stopped working and stood as immobile as stone staring at the flames, his eyes wide and glistening like crystals. I was scared he was having an apoplectic fit and went up to him. I grabbed his arms, which were hanging at his sides like foreign bodies, and said, "Pokri, my brother, what's wrong? Speak to me."

He answered in a low whisper, as if talking to himself, "To satisfy that fire three bodies must be burnt."

"What are you saying?" I shouted, frightened.

He was silent and continued gazing at the fire with the same terrifying look.

I shook him, "Pokri, speak to me!" and I took him by the jaw trying to turn his head towards me and away from the fire, which seemed to be hypnotising him. I was overcome by terror. I've always been afraid of people who are silent and say little. I'd observed that they were capable of the finest actions, or the vilest ones.

"Pokri, look at me. Maybe Siranush...?" I couldn't go

on. I embraced him like a father whose child was in danger and stared at him waiting for that crazy look to leave his eyes.

He began very slowly to move his arms, then suddenly grabbed my hands and spoke as though scared of hearing his own voice, "You're crying Stavri."

"Yes, I'm crying for you and Siranush. If you believe in our friendship, don't despair. We'll find a way to end this ordeal."

I led him to sit down on a pile of iron. He let me treat him like a sick person and in a short while spoke, "There's no other solution. I'll kill him and then we'll kill ourselves... who wants such a life..."

"What are you saying?" I roared, leaping to my feet, "You'd lose your lives and happiness for a bastard like that! Think straight, the right thing is to find a way to get that so-called tough guy off our backs without blood and big trouble, by giving him a lesson he'll never forget."

He looked at me, his eyes clear now, "Yes Stavri, yes."

The next day I went straight round to Dikran's workshop. He was alone with his apprentice Nedjip, and after a dry "Merhaba — Hello," I said straight out: "Listen Dikran. Stop this harm you're doing to Siranush and Pokris. Leave them alone or you'll have to deal with me!"

"What are you saying man?" he said mockingly, "Are you trying to scare me? Are you that interested? Maybe you're both sharing the whore? Ah, my poor fellow, I'll take her from you. Make her mine and enjoy her in front of your eyes. Am I going to take your threats seriously, you son of a bitch?"

Although I was boiling with rage at his insults, I kept cool and added drily, "Leave them alone, I tell you!" And I left without paying any attention to his reply. I was pleased because Nedjip had smiled at me secretly when he heard what I said.

After that incident things went on somewhat more peacefully; especially on the part of Kior-Eliza who didn't put so much pressure on Siranush as before and allowed her more peace. Pokris told me all the details, because after the day in front of the fire he had great faith in me. It was as though he no longer considered me a crazy and indifferent youth. Dikran limited the provocations and activities of his apprentices and friends around our workshop and he avoided us, particularly me. He never even passed in front of our door. It was as if he wanted to forget the whole matter. However, I didn't like that quietness, it seemed to me suspicious, like the calm before a storm which doesn't allow you to take precautions, as you can't tell from where the danger will come. I took measures to protect the three of us, but only in the area round the foundry because I thought that's where the trouble would break out. So, quite a time passed without me being able to uncover what Dikran's plan might be, hard as I tried.

. . .

Until one night on my way back home from Yeni Şehir, where I'd been drinking heavily with some friends. I was cutting across some empty building plots when I noticed a shadow lurking near a low wall. It was a sweet autumn night, not very dark and the shape reminded me of Nedjip, although that seemed impossible to me as the young Turk lived at the other end of the Great City at Yedi Koule. Then I remembered his words at the café. I looked carefully all around and pulled out my blackjack, a wired, short whip weighted with lead, which I always had hidden in my wide cummerbund. I didn't see or hear anything but continued straight towards the place where I had seen the shadow:

"Nedjip!" I shouted hoarsely, but the shadow disappeared behind the wall.

I lengthened my stride to pass the wall and reach the open ground beyond, looking all around me as I went. Suddenly, from a little behind me on my right, a man, who'd been hiding behind a pile of rubbish and earth, threw himself violently at me snorting like a wild animal. He held high a large, gleaming knife. It was Dikran.

"It's you is it, you rat!" I grunted and managed to whack him hard with the blackjack on the arm which held the knife.

"Ach! Bastard!" he almost screamed as the knife flew from his hand. His arm fell to his side as if broken and he grabbed it with his other hand, groaning. Without wasting a second I launched myself at him, kicking and punching. He fell, spread-eagled to the ground and I threw myself on him. At that moment I became aware of another shadow on the right of the wall, standing motionless as if awaiting the result of the struggle.

Sitting on top of Dikran, I squeezed his waist tightly between my knees, holding his undamaged left arm across his body with my left hand. His other arm lay by his side like that of a dead man. I had my right hand tightly round his throat and bashed his head against the ground, growling through gritted teeth:

"I could slaughter you like a pig, but won't dirty my hands on shit like you! You disgust me and I spit on you!"

He struggled to break free from the grasp of my legs and hands and lashed around like a fish in a net. For a moment, I raised my head and glanced towards where I had seen the shadows, but saw nothing there, nor all around me.

Suddenly, I felt a burning blow on my left arm. Dikran had grabbed the knife with his damaged hand and with a super-human effort managed to stab me. Before I could act to forestall a second blow, his arm fell back beside him as though he were paralysed, his hand opened, and the knife fell to the ground. His head was still in my hand like a rubber ball which I could do what I liked with, without resistance. His body stopped moving completely and his legs tensed stiffly. It seemed to me he had fainted. He didn't even groan. I stopped bashing his head on the ground and raised his left arm, which I'd been holding tightly against his belly; it fell back limply. I partly released my fingers from round his throat but was ready to tighten them again in case he was pretending to have fainted and would suddenly throw himself on me and knife me again when I thought I was finished with him. His head didn't move. He was really out. But I didn't think he could be dead as I hadn't squeezed his throat hard enough to kill him. I'd only ground his head into the earth.

When I saw him in that condition, not sure if he was dead or alive, I got up off him to leave. Let come to him what may; he deserved it. The blood flowed hot from the wound in my arm in thick drops like a dripping tap. I had no time to look at my wound. I took my sleeve and wound it as tightly as I could round my arm, from shoulder to wrist, tying it with a handkerchief at the bottom to stop the blood from dripping. The wound stung and burned, yet the bloody sleeve felt cold against my flesh and I was dizzy from the tension of the struggle and the coolness of the night. Before I left, I had a good look around to make sure I hadn't dropped anything. Then I noticed the fingers of my right hand, which had been clutching Dikran's neck, were covered in blood. I was taken by surprise but didn't stop to discover the reason; I thought it had probably happened while I was binding up my wounded arm.

I changed direction several times and finally arrived at a friend's house in a neighbourhood far from my own. It was well past midnight. My friend, who was used to such late-night visits, opened the door sleepy-eyed, murmured a welcome and went back to bed. I simply told him I was drunk and went straight into the kitchen, where I rinsed my clothes carefully to get rid of every trace of blood. I placed tobacco over my wound and bound it with the handkerchief, lay down and slept for a while, got up before dawn had fully broken, and left.

I went straight to Kalphas, a village further on from Kayit Hane up from the Golden Horn, a peaceful village of well-tended market-gardens; a secret refuge for Greeks who had dealings with the authorities. The next day, I sent a friend who sold fruit in the streets, but who also carried out other business, to Sinem Köy to learn any news. I expected that Dikran had made an accusation against me and that the police would have been to my house, and the houses of my family, and turned them upside down. Christeas, for that was his name, first went to the centre of the village to see if there was any news, but there was none. He then went to my place, supposedly to sell fresh fruit, and was told that nobody had come looking for me. As for my absence, nobody was uneasy because they knew my habits. Christeas didn't reveal anything to anybody.

On the second day he went to the workshop. Again, there was nothing suspicious, though they were uneasy about my absence; especially Pokris who was worried because, as he said to Christeas, Dikran hadn't been to his foundry for two days, but remained closed up at home, saying he was ill. Nobody knew anything about me as it seemed Dikran hadn't said a word to anyone about the incident and had forbidden the others who were with him to talk.

To reassure Pokris, Christeas told him only where I was and that I was lightly wounded. When he returned to Kalphas he gave me all the news and said that, based on what he'd verified, he'd come to the conclusion that Dikran hadn't reported me to the police. However, I had no faith in the Armenian and expected them to come for me any day now. So I remained at the village until my wound had healed. Pokris would arrange, through Christeas, to keep me informed of what was going on.

After a few days, Dikran came out of his house with his throat bandaged. He went straight to our workshop before visiting his own. When Pokris came face to face with him, he was bewildered. It wasn't the Dikran he knew, the aggressive, so-called "tough guy." He had changed. He looked downcast; his expression pained. He looked like a decent young man. He went straight to Pokris, extended his hand and said, "Pokris, my brother, let me kiss you with the kiss of true friendship..."

Pokris gave him his hand mechanically and, as if hypnotised, allowed Dikran to kiss him. The other craftsmen and apprentices had stopped working and watched the scene in silent amazement, Mastro-Pandias among them.

"Tell me, Pokris, where is Stavris? I want to thank him

for saving me. There's not a better man than him. From now on I'll look on him as more than a brother." And his eyes filled with tears.

Pokris said he didn't know where I was and asked what was behind this whole performance. Dikran then told him in a few words what had happened between us and repeated that he needed to see me.

Later, Pokris sent me a message informing me of Dikran's behaviour and saying that I could now return. The good man believed in the Armenian's sincerity. I didn't go but sent Christeas to Dikran to tell him I was waiting for him. He agreed to come to Kalphas the same day. As soon as he saw me, he ran forward, took my hands in his and, before I could prevent him, kissed me, saying with tears in his eyes, "My brother Stavri, instead of killing me you saved me!"

He embraced me and kissed me warmly. His words and manner moved me, and I slapped him on the back and invited him to sit down.

But he remained standing and continued: "Let me tell you that you treated me better than my father or brother. Forgive me Stavri, for what I've done up to now. I was a no-gooder and you've made me a man."

And he started to cry like a child. I took him by the shoulders and kissed him, "Don't worry, from now on we'll be the best of friends."

"Is that true Stavri?" he shouted; his eyes full of tears of joy now.

After we'd sat down, I brought out a bottle of rakı and

filled two glasses; we toasted each other's health and downed them in one go. Then I asked him, smiling, "Well tell me now, what happened after our fight? You had fainted; I knew you weren't dead as I'd only hit you on the arm with my blackjack. Did your lads help you?"

"No way!" he laughed, "They were terrified and left so fast nobody could have caught them. But let me tell you from the beginning. After a lot of thought, I'd decided to deal with you first and get you out of the way; I could easily handle Pokris later. So, I set my lads to watch you closely. Where you went, what you did, where you slept. That lasted quite a while and was tedious. It made me nervous, but I had to grit my teeth and wait for the right moment to finish with you. So that night we followed you to the tavern at Yeni Şehir. I waited for you to leave and worked out a plan to deal with you that very night. I knew the area well. I'd follow you from a distance and strike at the right moment. When I saw you cutting across those building plots I smiled at my good luck. It was the perfect lonely spot. I increased my pace to get in front of you and stationed my lads so they could come to help me if things didn't go well. I hid crouching behind the pile of rubbish and attacked you as you passed. But when you threw me down, I fell on a broken bottle which stuck in the back of my neck, luckily slightly to the side, and every time you banged my head on the ground the glass went in further and blood gushed out. I was near fainting and gathered all my strength to stab you once with the arm you had crippled with the blackjack, because you had my other arm trapped. Then I fainted with the glass stuck in my neck. The cold of the night brought me round after a while. I was trembling all over. With great difficulty I pulled myself to my feet. The broken bottle lay on the ground and the blood was running hot down my back. I squeezed the wound shut with my hand. It was burning painfully, but I managed to bind it as tightly as I could with my handkerchief to stop the blood flowing. I also took off my cummerbund and tied it round my throat. I was furious because of my failure and the terrible state I was in. I cursed you and threatened you, swore I'd kill you wherever I found you and let them take me to the gallows. The hand you had hit with the blackjack was hurting and I remembered the knife. I searched around and found it on the ground. Then I started heading straight to the police station to bring a charge against you. It was very difficult to walk because I didn't have control of my legs. I felt very weak and my whole body was burning like it was wounded. My guts were on fire, but my flesh was shaking as if freezing water had been thrown over me. My throat was dry, and I was so thirsty I'd have drunk muddy water. Before I reached the police station, I threw the knife into an empty plot and, I don't know why—it's a mystery—hid my money in my shoe.

But when I went into the police station and saw the mugs of all those Turkish coppers, with their fezes, their swords, their guns and the emblem of the Sultan on the wall—like a huge black spider you'd think was going to eat you—I froze. A sudden thought struck me. What was I going to do? Inform on the man who had saved my life? Who had left me alive despite my treachery? I made as if to leave, but it was too late. A policeman approached me.

'What's happened to you? Where are you going?' he shouted.

I had the inspiration, maybe it was the truth, to pretend to be ill and fell to the ground. Two other coppers ran over and pulled me to my feet.

'Water,' I whispered weakly. They sat me in a chair and brought me a carafe of water. I drank more than a glassful. When I had come around a little, they began the interrogation: What? How? Where? I gave them name, address, profession—not the real ones. Said how I'd been going home drunk, that's why I couldn't remember anything except that two unknown attackers had fallen on me, taken my money and left me unconscious. The only true part of my statement was that the wound had been caused by a broken bottle and that I had passed out. When I had finished, the chief officer asked me drily if I suspected anyone. I said 'no' and added that it was a usual sort of attack by petty thieves, the evidence being that they hadn't wounded me deliberately. I thanked Allah that the bottle had only given me a flesh wound as it could have gone into my brain and left me dead on the spot. 'Kısmet,' said the Big-Copper, and assured me, yawning, they'd do what was necessary to arrest the criminals and would inform me as soon as they had news. I bowed, complimented him on his diligence, thanked him and got up to leave. Good man that he was, he said he could see I was in a bad way and that I could sleep at the station in the hammock of one of the policemen, or if I insisted on leaving, he would get one of his men to escort me home so I would come to no more harm. Terrified, and with a frozen smile on my lips, I assured him I was absolutely fine and, thanking him again, I finally managed to get away."

The same day, to the amazement of all our colleagues, Dikran and I went down to the workshops together. And that evening, together with Pokris and Siranush, we all ate together at his house, where his mother couldn't do enough for us, especially after her son told her I had saved him from a great danger. Dikran made it clear, with his words and actions, that he wanted us to forget the past. We ate and drank like good, old friends who had met again after a long time.

And the very next day he went to sort out Siranush's problem with Kior-Eliza. But the cunning *lecha* smelt something was up and did not consent easily. She feared that if Dikran's rage at Siranush ended, she would no longer be able to enjoy herself in cultivating his hatred for the girl. However Dikran, partly by sweet-talking and partly with a pimp's toughness, managed to get her to agree to a reasonable sum to pay off the debt; though, even then, it was a higher price than the usual one. Pokris and

Siranush agreed to it, so as to be free of the whole story for once and for all. They put together all their savings, and together with a small loan from Mastro-Pandias, made up the sum. Dikran, at a moment when he'd beguiled the old hag with his erotic sweet-talk and before she had time to regret it, immediately brought in a notary, gave her the money, got her to sign the paper and Siranush was free.

She left the *kerhane* that very evening. The other girls and the rest of the staff saw her off like a bride with good wishes, tears and presents. Even Kior-Eliza was shamed into giving something and presented her with an old tray and five liqueur glasses, three of them cracked.

A few days later the wedding took place in a room a friend of ours had lent them until they could find a place of their own to rent. Dikran and I were the *koumbari* or "best men" with Dikran's mother and Mastro-Pandias as guests. I've been to many weddings in my life, both rich and poor, but none could compare in simple beauty and pure joy to the wedding of Pokris and Siranush. In that small, almost bare room, the simply dressed newly-weds shone with happiness and purity like two virgin youngsters as they stole happy, pride-filled glances at each other and smiled gratefully at us.

After the wedding their greatest wish was to have a child. Siranush consulted midwives, even doctors. She prayed to male and female saints and took the waters at Bursa; and after two years they had a little boy. Pokris, who had a little education, chose the name Simon because it's the same in both Armenian and Greek. But Dikran and his parents called him "Küçük Stavri," as we would say in Greek "Stavraki" or "Little Stavri." Dikran and I were often round at their house until, after some time, I left for Greece. After that, I learned from the faithful Dikran's letters that Pokris and Siranush remained as much in love as ever and produced a line of children as beautiful as they were themselves.

SIX

Pervelis

One day Pervelis turned up at the *teke*, the hash-den where we hung out. He wore a black frock coat, striped trousers and a hard Mirabeau hat. He had just returned from Paris, where he had been for five years; the first two with breaks in Constantinople and the last three continuously. He was there for "medical studies," so said his father, Mr Pantzaridis, a doctor from Psomathia, or Samatia, as the Turks call it; from the name "The Gate of Psamathou," which is found in a neighbourhood of The City at the southern end of the Byzantine walls by the Sea of Marmara. He wanted his only child, Hippocratis Pantzaridis, for such was his name, to become a doctor with a gold plate on his door reading: "Doctor from Paris."

But Pervelis—as all his friends had nicknamed him—went to Paris with that name, and "Pervelis" he returned. He had learned a few things in Paris: to drink absinthe, to pawn whatever passed through his hands, be it his own or another's, to borrow money and not repay it, even though his father was always sending him money for his "scientific education." When the five years of his student days were over, his father sent him "the new doctor's return-fare," which Pervelis managed to spend to the last sou on farewell parties with his pals and girlfriends in the Latin Quarter. To pay his fare home, he sold all his books and whatever else he could, keeping only the frock coat and the Mirabeau. He forgot, however, to bring home his diploma since he had "come up against a snag with that arteriosclerotic old spinster the Ècole de Medicine," as he used to say.

Soon after arriving in The City, he came around to the *teke* to find his old companions, accompanied by one or two friends he had come across at other hangouts. He entered the *teke* as if at home. The *hasiklides* or hash-smokers known and unknown, welcomed him joyfully; from every side was heard "Welcome" and "Hoş geldin"; one or two even said "Welcome your eminence," as they used to greet the doctors. Pervelis, moved by his welcome, greeted and thanked all his old friends. The "Usta" prepared the *nargiles* with special care, while Pervelis watched the behaviour of the regulars with respectful attention and tried to copy them. He wanted to show that, even though he had been away for so long, he had remained faithful to the customs of the country and was still a strong smoker. He paid for everybody and spent freely.

After smoking for quite a while, we decided to go

somewhere else to meet other friends. When Pervelis stood up he was well and truly high. He staggered and mixed up his words. His condition grew worse as his high hadn't "come around," but he wouldn't allow anyone to help him keep his balance. When we got out into the yard, he jumped onto a table and shouted: "I'll fly, I'll fly!" ready to jump anywhere. With difficulty, we managed to restrain him, and seeing the state he was in decided to take him home rather than to a wine house or café. On the way there Pervelis walked heavily and silently, but every now and then he shouted: "I want to fly. I'll fly!"

He tried hard to escape from our grasp. Someone said that we shouldn't take him home in this condition, especially since he had only just got back from Paris. He suggested we go and hang out at Mehmet Reis's café at Gümüşsuyu (Silverwaters), where not many people went. There it was always cool, and Pervelis would be able to drink his coffee quietly and eat some sweet caramel-pudding to bring him round. Everybody liked the idea and we set off...

The café's position was one of the most beautiful in Constantinople. Often the simplest people know best where to build their *konak*, their mansion, no matter how small and poor it may be, and offer sweet-smelling coffee in places with a view that fills the soul with joy and delight. From Mehmet Reis's place you could see much of the Boundless City with its many beauties: on the left the wavy Bosphorus with its green hills and the soft outlines of its colourful suburbs. On the right the Golden Horn, wide and silver-green. In front of the café, the buzzing European side of the city spread out in tiers and was reflected in the playing waters of the Great Harbour full of ships, some anchored, others gliding through the waves. Beyond, rose ancient Byzantium, The City of the Greeks, with its ruins, its marble walls running along the shore, Agia Sophia and the other great mosques with their minarets rising over the seven hills. To the left of the harbour lay Scutari, which became a true "Golden City" when the setting sun was reflected on its windows; and in the far distance the eye could make out the rose-coloured outline of the mountains of Asia Minor with the Princes Islands scattered before them across the waters of the Sea of Marmara.

On the side of the café facing that beautiful view there was something like a platform, in front of which was a steep slope. This platform was roofed with a *tsardi*, branches which Mehmet Reis always kept fresh and green, throwing the old, dried-out ones down the slope. The platform, which had a low wall built round its edges wide enough to sit on, jutted out over the steep drop like a headland and caught the fresh breezes which blew either from Kayit Hane and the Golden Horn on the right, or from the Bosphorus on the left.

Our group spread out on the platform under the *tsardi* and ordered coffee, caramel pudding and cool water from the spring of Gümüşsuyu. Pervelis appeared calm. He sat with his head bent heavily forward, as if sleepy. We helped him drink his coffee and eat his pudding. At one moment he suddenly raised his head and saw the glorious view. His eyes grew wide and his mouth opened as if to shout. He remained like that for a few moments, then suddenly rushed forward and jumped on to the low wall shouting:

"I'll fly! I'll fly! I can't stand it any more, I'll fly!"

One or two of us made as if to run and grab him, but Govitzas, a great joker, stopped them:

"Let him fly if he wants to." He turned towards Pervelis and continued, "Go on fly. Let's see you."

The latter then opened his arms wide, flapped them like wings, weakly and slowly, and shouting out, "Look, I'm flying! I'm flying!" threw himself into space with his head thrust out and his body twisted like an awkward swimmer taking a dive. We all rushed forward, some terrified, others laughing. When we reached the edge we saw Pervelis rolling over and over down the slope; legs flying one way, arms another, like a parcel that had come untied. His Mirabeau hat, as if made of rubber, was bumping down the slope in front of him, leading the way. One or two of us who knew the area, along with some Turkish customers, started running down the narrow path which wound its way down the hill. We managed to catch up with Pervelis and gather him together. The rest watched from above and Mehmet Reis muttered over and over, "Vay, vay, ach zavallı — the poor fellow, the poor fellow."

. . .

They carried him back up to the coffeehouse. His frock coat was torn, his hands grazed, his face bruised. Covered in earth and rubbish that had stuck to him as he rolled, he was well and truly battered. His Mirabeau they hadn't saved; it must have rolled the whole way down to the sea at Kabataş. He was lucky that the earth on the slope was soft and wet from the recent spring rains and not stony. Otherwise, he could have been really badly injured, if not killed. All of us realised that, and bitterly regretted what had happened; but the harm was done.

Pervelis was pale and unconscious. They laid him down on three tables pushed together to make a bed, with our jackets thrown over it to make it soft. Poor Pervelis was in pain and labouring for breath. We all tried affectionately to comfort him. One placed a handkerchief soaked in rakı and water over his face to relieve the pain of the bruising. Two washed his hands. Others cleaned his clothing, friends and strangers together. Mehmet Reis placed a bottle of vinegar under his nose and rubbed his neck. So we brought him round and got him to drink some cognac mixed with water. But when we wanted to take him home, we found ourselves in difficulty. There were no carriages around in that isolated spot. A couple of us went to the local Fire Station of Gümüşsuyu to see if they had a *sedye* —one of the old-time sedan chairs that were still used in those days, even if rarely—but they didn't have one. We tried tying together two of the café's benches to make a stretcher, but it was too clumsy and heavy.

. . .

In the meantime, some gypsies, who had their cabin nearby and made a living selling the junk people threw down the slope, got wind of what was going on and appeared at the café with a large pannier of the type used to carry vegetables at the market. They suggested that we put Pervelis inside and carry it hanging from a long, thick pole which they would hoist onto their shoulders by the two ends. Fortunately, some Turks from the neighbourhood had the idea to go to the local police station and borrow a stretcher that was used to carry the injured and the dead. We laid Pervelis on it and made him as comfortable as possible after tending his wounds as well as we could and cleaning his clothes. Mehmet Reis put a cushion under his head and we covered him with two sacks to hide the condition of his frock coat. Pervelis had come round and was no longer dizzy. The poor fellow complained though, that he was sore all over his body. We consoled him and tried to encourage him, gave him cognac, coffee and caramel pudding all together, teased him and made jokes, while he laughed and groaned at the same time.

Finally, all together, we set off to carry him home; one of us holding the stretcher at the head end, another at the foot. We went very slowly, for at every jolt Pervelis complained that he was in pain. Every now and then we changed position and those who were not carrying spread out, right and left, laughing and joking. Someone asked Pervelis what he'd seen up there when he was flying. Another, who was a bit of a singer and rhymester began singing in a psalm-like way to the tune of *In the Mountains There So High*, and in time with the steps of the stretcher bearers:

Up there high in the sky
Pervelis thought that he would fly
In his right hand he held
For a sceptre a loulas

Some held the bass drone, as in a church, while others sang in chorus; the rest, Pervelis too, laughing wholeheartedly as we continued on our way.

SEVEN

Loukas the Oil-Seller

He came from a village lost in the high mountains of Thrace where the inhabitants had to leave home from childhood in order to make a living elsewhere or remain on that infertile ground and die young. He was a pedlar, or as he put it a "merchant" who sold olive-oil in the poor neighbourhoods. From dawn till night, winter and summer, he left no alley uncovered, even in the furthest districts, shouting his wares in a nasal voice. Not one syllable could be made out, but everyone knew it was him; a grouchy, suspicious-minded person who spoke little and was always in a hurry but was regular and methodical in his work.

On his back, he carried two tin containers filled with oil, on a framework he had made himself. It hung over his shoulders from two strong leather straps across his chest and was supported by a sort of saddle above his buttocks. Two copper measures, one of 50 drams the other of 100, rang at his side like bells. Each of the tin containers had a tap which stuck forward at his sides. Long necked as a stork, he would turn his head like a puppet, his eyes narrowed, and fill the measures without spilling a drop. The larger the amount bought, the more carefully he would pour the oil into the customer's bottle, always cheating by keeping just a little bit back for himself. The right-hand container supposedly contained the best quality oil, the left the second-rate, but in fact it was the same in both and Loukas knew how to dilute it and stretch it with his alchemy.

He always wore the same clothes, splattered with oil and heavily patched by himself. Even his body was oil-splattered from top to bottom. He only changed his clothes at Christmas and at Easter, when he put on his good suit—once black but now worn out and turned a shiny black-green by time. Then he went to the hammam; otherwise he didn't wash. His official name was Loukas the Oilman. But people called him "Oily" and the children in the street shouted "Oil-Rat" whenever he passed.

Above all, he was a fanatical miser. You'd rarely see him eating at midday. He loved money more than he did his life and would nibble on a little bit of the dry bread which he kept tucked underneath his armpit as he passed through the neighbourhoods, anxious not to miss a single customer and to sell as much oil as possible. In the evening, when his work was over, his appearance changed; he looked terrified, as if in danger of losing the treasure he had on him, the day's takings. Late, when it grew dark, he took the road home, the road to his shack. He would lean forward, his arms tightly crossed over his chest, where he had hidden the money, and hold the two copper measures tightly together with one hand, so they wouldn't rattle and betray his passing. He bent low to make himself as small as possible, so as not to be easily recognised, and every night took a different route through the alleyways. He would even pass right through the village, as if he had moved his abode, and only double back to the shack after dark. So it was night when he returned to his refuge, unobserved—as he believed.

However, before he left the *çarşı*, the marketplace, he dined. For a few coppers, he bought half a loaf of dry bread, squeezed it tightly under his armpit, and laden down with the containers on his back, entered some *lokanta*, or a wine house which also offered food. He went up to the counter where the dishes were displayed, smelling appetisingly and gleaming with sauces. He would look at them greedily, his eyes popping, and ask in a trembling, hoarse voice:

"What's good today mastora?"

The cook, for his own amusement, would slowly name the dishes and recite their virtues as if he had his most gourmet customer before him:

"We have, my dear, aubergine moussaka you would begrudge sharing even with your own kids...some liver with oregano you could eat till you burst...baked bonito with plenty of garlic. You'd rather divorce your sensitive wife, who is disgusted by garlic, than deprive yourself of the pleasure of this delicacy..." deliberately referring to the most appetising dishes while dipping a spoon in one, a fork in another, as if preparing to serve them.

Loukas lent over the stew-pots drawing in the aromas of the food and breaking off pieces of the stale bread he carried with him. Breathing in deeply, he chewed on the pieces once or twice and then swallowed them virtually whole with a spasmodic movement like a hiccup. He did this in two or three restaurants where the bosses put up with him because they enjoyed teasing him. So he enjoyed a dinner of food-smells and dry bread, but always kept one bit of the latter back for the next morning's snack. This performance went on every evening and after such a filling meal Loukas would disappear. Nobody ever saw him in a café or a wine house or ever came across him anywhere else. He became invisible.

One evening, a couple of no-gooders who were broke and on the look out for some fun thought: "What about the Oil-Rat? He must have some cash on him."

They followed him, stalked him until they finally saw him entering a wooden shack. You could only just make it out amongst the broken-down storerooms, long grass and undergrowth in the wild orchard of a large ruined mansion beyond the village. That's where Loukas holed up, slipping through a small door which he half-opened silently, looking around him like a hunted cat. The two who'd smelt him out waited to see some light appear from inside, but none came. The shack had no window, not even a hole. "What a miser! Not even a light!" one whispered to the other, "He must've got used to seeing in the dark, like an owl." They approached silently and circled the shack but couldn't find a crack wide enough to look through; even the keyhole was dark. It was as if nobody was there. One of them took out a knife and slowly pushed the blade into one of the thin slits in the old planks. There wasn't much resistance and when he carefully pulled it out a line of light appeared, thin as a golden hair. He almost let out a hoarse curse of triumph but stifled it quickly. He repeated the experiment with great care and skill and in a short while had made the slit wide enough to reveal the Oil-Rat's secret.

Loukas had pulled aside an old heavy chest and placed an oil-lamp on it. He then lifted up a rag-rug, knelt down and began digging feverishly at the earth floor with his hands. Every so often, he paused and looked around him as if some enemy might suddenly appear from among the variety of stuff that surrounded him: rags, old straw-mats, paper, lint and old cotton which hung from the wooden walls of the shack to cover the cracks and on which the dim light of the flickering lamp created goblin-like shadows. After a few minutes, he carefully withdrew a padlocked metal box from the pit which he had opened.

He sat cross-legged and placed the box on his lap as if it were a beloved, living creature, then took from his breast a key, which hung from his neck on a leather cord, and with trembling hands opened it. A faint glow lit up his thin face as it twitched with unnatural joy. He thrust his hands in, drew out some gold coins, brought them close to his startled eyes and examined them as if making sure they were real before more calmly replacing them. Following this, he began removing coins one or two at a time, scrutinising them in the lamplight. He turned them from one side to another, moved them up and down as if he were watching them dance, his bulging eyes shining greedily. Then he placed some inside his clothing, against his flesh and hugged them with his arms crossed over his breast swaying left and right, up and down murmuring a tune quietly, like a lullaby to a child, while his face, ravaged by deprivation, was distorted by almost demonic grimaces. After a while, he removed the coins from his breast, examined them carefully again and returned them one by one to the box, counting in a whisper. Having placed them inside, he suddenly became uneasy and agitated, removed them all, counted them one by one on his palm and, finally satisfied, dropped them slowly back into the box, leaning forward exultantly to hear their low ringing as they fell.

He padlocked his money box, and after verifying countless times that it was truly secure, dug the pit a little deeper, caressed the box tenderly and carefully laid it down. He covered it with earth which he patted down with his hands, then stood up and trod it down, taking small steps in a tight circle as if performing some clumsy, heavy dance. Finally, he spread the rag-rug, placed the wooden chest on top of it and sat down wearily with a satisfied, idiotic smile. The thieves didn't need any more details, they had seen enough.

The next day, Loukas the Oilman made his usual rounds of the poor neighbourhoods selling as much oil as he could, then secured his takings against his breast, ate heartily of food smells and stale bread and returned, taking all precautions, to his shack. There, however, unexpected disaster awaited him. When he lit the oil-lamp everything was in order and he carried out the usual ritual opening of his tin treasure-chest. Only to find it empty except for a misspelt note written on a piece of torn packing paper in capital letters: LOST SOLE—COZ YOU DON NO HOW TO INJOY YOR GOLD WE TUK IT TO HAV A GOOD TIME AT YOR EKSPENSE...it was signed with two clumsy crosses.

Loukas didn't suffer apoplexy or lose his mind, but he went through terrible moments as if experiencing the agonies of death. In the first minutes of despair he wanted to harm himself; then he became wild with the desire for revenge, to kill someone, but who? In his fury he suspected the whole village. Black thoughts, terrifying schemes and despairing decisions assailed his confused mind. His blood was boiling. He fixed his bulging eyes wildly on the dark corners of the shack as if seeking to reveal something that could help him find his treasure and be saved from this ordeal. Then he began to search the place, as if he'd hidden the treasure himself and forgotten where. Every so often, a despairing "Ach" or a grieving "Och" escaped from his guts. He clenched his fists wildly as if throttling the thieves. But he didn't swear nor call on the saints for help, nor shed a tear. Eventually, drained by that distressing paroxysm, he sat down on the chest gazing at the empty money-box he'd thrown into the pit. In a short while, sleep overcame him.

When he awoke, he was aching all over as if he'd been tortured and was too exhausted to get up or think straight. He looked around heavy-eyed and remained sitting for quite some time until slowly he began to recover the use of his limbs and to remember, confusedly, where he was and what had happened. A thin yellow flame from the burnt down wick of the oil-lamp threw a dim light and his eyes were drawn to the pit with the empty iron money box, its lid open and gaping like a black, toothless mouth. He stared at it, his chest tightening as though he were suffocating and unable to catch his breath. Suddenly, he stood up, staggered to the door and threw it wide-open. A relieving "Ach" lightened his chest as he deeply drew in the early morning air, gazing at the sweetly breaking dawn.

He stood there uncertainly, his face still dark and grim, then turned and looked back inside the shack. The dim dawn light fell first on the oil-containers, causing them to glisten joyfully. Loukas looked them over as if remembering something. Suddenly a need, unknown to him until then, impelled him to go over to the amphora which held his drinking-water and pour some of the contents over his head. With swift movements he rubbed his face, throat and arms, wetting his clothes in the process. He shivered as he felt his burning brain and body cooling down. Without drying himself, wet as he was, he approached the containers. He appeared wide-awake and seemed to have taken some decision, as if that water had re-baptised him. He loaded himself up with all his equipment, patting himself to make sure he had forgotten nothing, then walked steadily to the open doorway, crossed the threshold with a jump and closed the door behind him with a backwards kick. He set off walking fast and unsteadily without knowing clearly where he was headed, like a man made drunk by that cool rose-coloured dawn with its sweet scent of spring.

It seemed to him that the first low village houses, humble and clean, were waiting to greet him and his voice, which issued from his dry throat, hoarse and trembling. The housewives heard him and came to their doors with bottles in hand, but his unusual appearance surprised them:

"What's happened to him?"

"Something strange by the look of him!"

"The Oil-Rat's in love! It's clear as can be from the look on his face! And do you know who with? With the daughter of the old seven-titted bitch!"

And they all burst out laughing.

The teasing and joking went on from lane to lane

while Loukas served them without saying a word, "Struck dumb by love," the gossips chuckled. He looked bewilderedly from one to another and when his eye fell on somebody good-looking, he laughed like a child. In the midst of all this female coquetry and teasing he felt oppressed by embarrassment, but at the same time wanted to throw off that feeling and take part in the fun.

He continued making his way through the alleys and lanes, carried along by the habits of his work, not anxiously as before but with a feeling of lightness and calm. It was strange; it was no longer the desire for gain that drew him on, but the people with their jokes, antics and chat. He began to reflect on the disaster that had befallen him more calmly; to consider that all the people he met on his rounds might have suffered who knows what in the course of their lives but said nothing about it. Until the evening he continued his round of the neighbourhoods, saying nothing to a soul about his terrible misfortune. He tried hard to put it out of his mind and became so absorbed in his work that by the end of the day he hadn't thought of it for several hours. But he couldn't dine as before on food smells and dry bread and his stomach felt as if it had received a heavy blow, a punch which had shaken his bony frame.

The next day and the next, and from then on, Loukas continued to work regularly, closed however, in a stubborn silence which had a sort of modest dignity about it. He didn't want to know who had carried out the evil act which had both dangerously disrupted his life but also saved him. Nor did he go to the police and take out a summons against

"Persons Unknown." Who would have believed him? Who would have stood witness for the grimy "Oil-Rat" who cheated everyone with his poor-quality oil, and even more, with his measures? People would be pleased to hear of his disaster and laugh at the clever way his golden pounds had been lifted. If the no-gooders had mentioned it, it would have been to some of their trusted friends who had joined in on the partying they'd been enjoying while spending the Oilman's gold. Though, they were surprised that the miser hadn't said a word to anyone about the dirty trick that had been played on him and asked each other, a little uneasily, what sort of a weird person they were dealing with. It was a strange thing...

But it didn't remain a mystery for long. Unexpectedly, early one afternoon, Loukas the Oilman was seen sitting in the shade of a wall eating; not, as before, stale bread, but good fresh bread with tomatoes and olives, and after that he bit into an apple. Even more strangely, he was wearing different clothes; also old and patched, but not oil spattered. Then one evening people witnessed a miracle. Loukas entered one of the restaurants where he used to dine on food smells and stale bread. He didn't even have his containers on his back and wasn't carrying any stale bread. He was poorly dressed, but clean. He sat down discretely at a corner table and waited. When the boss saw him in this new guise he approached and asked, almost politely, what he wanted. Loukas answered calmly with an open smile: "To eat like a human being whatever food you bring me, cause I know you're a good cook."

The spectacle continued before the startled eyes of the other customers. They didn't look at their own plates but watched out of the corners of their eyes as Loukas took his time eating and drinking his wine with good appetite. When he had finished, he paid his bill, left a tip for the boy who served the tables and made for the door. The lad was so amazed he abandoned his work, and with bulging eyes, followed Loukas silently to the door. There he managed to mumble the words "thank you" in a weak voice like a eunuch's. The boy's behaviour was a reflection of the amazement felt by all who had seen the Oil-Rat eat like a human being.

Now Loukas's life changed radically, took on a new rhythm. He continued to spend his days going around the neighbourhoods, but no longer like a hunted dog.

He shouted his wares in a voice as clear as a bell, like a skilful cantor. He sold better quality oil and didn't dilute it. In the evenings he returned to his shack by the most direct route without taking any precautions.

There, he washed, removed his work clothes and put on others, patched but clean; then returned to the village to sit and chat with company. Everyone was astounded by this metamorphosis and could no longer recognise in him Loukas the Oilman, the grimy Oil-Rat. Now that he'd cleaned himself up, he'd begun a new life—become another person. His face was tranquil and open, no longer fierce and dark, his glance not dull and fearful, but bright and bold. He stroked his moustache proudly with what seemed a joyful smile and his upright carriage and lithe gait made him attractive as he wasn't a bad looking man. Every detail about him now stirred the interest of the women and they wanted to know what had changed him so. They teased him saying he was dressing well and eating more to become handsome, to fortify himself, so he could find some soulmate and taste the joys of love.

Loukas was not annoyed by this, just smiled slyly and gave them answers that aroused their curiosity even more. No longer glum and tetchy, he was smiling, talkative and kindly, interested in seeking out and enjoying everything he had been deprived of before. He dallied at the doors of those who bought his oil to chat with the housewives and compliment them on their "charms which grew fresher every day," as he said. Among them, indeed, some middle-aged ones, a little the worse for wear, began to be interested in "Mr Loukas," as they now called him. They found him good-looking, even very manly, and they buttered him up to try to lure him into marriage. That's why they bought a little oil from him every day, to get him into conversation, not to tease him, but to make flirtatious remarks, their eyes shining, their bodies swaying and giggling so much you'd think someone was tickling them.

Loukas would please them by answering gallantly and with one generous movement empty his oil-measure to the very last drop. Often, while emptying a little extra oil into a good-looking woman's bottle he would say with feeling: "There you are, for your velvet eyes..." to another, looking at her lips: "Something for that carnation you have for a mouth to enjoy." Or to another flirtatious housewife he would whisper amorously, his eyes sparkling: "Your swaying hips deserve this."

He had learnt to enjoy every moment of the small pleasures that life brings. People now appreciated his jokes and teasing and called him "Loukas the Joker." His old nicknames were forgotten, and he was generally liked, while his clever jokes and teasing enlivened the monotonous life of the village and were the subject of much gossip.

He now had friends, several of them very close, whom he would meet in the wine houses to share a meze and clink glasses. Some offered to lend him money to extend his business; but Loukas—who had emerged strong from his terrible experience thanks to his Easterner's belief in "*kismet*," in destiny, and his in-born good sense—didn't want to lose his joyful freedom and peace of mind for all the riches in the world, and declined the offers. He spent what he had in his pocket, and that was the day's takings as he no longer saved even a cent. "May my ne'er-do-well heirs find nothing," he would say, laughing, as he had no relations in this world. Every evening, until late, he would eat, drink, sing and dance with his friends, spending as freely on them as they did on him. Sometimes, when he was a little drunk, they'd hear him murmur, as if confessing to someone: "They can have it! They can have it! The rats! Can you take it with you?" Then he would shout to the others: "Your health lads! Let's drink and enjoy ourselves.

Forget your worries!" and he'd begin his favourite song, beating his feet rhythmically on the floor: "Let's drink up and forget the black earth that will swallow us..."

The no-gooders, who in the meantime had spent every last one of Loukas's pounds, saw him so changed that they couldn't understand how the miracle had happened: Loukas the grimy Oilman who sold diluted oil, who cheated with the weights, the greasy Oil-Rat, the fanatical miser, had become a human being like them—carefree, good-humoured, a spender! They too, partied with him and bought him drinks whole-heartedly. From then on, the whole village officially called him "Mister Loukas the Oilman," as they referred to other oil-merchants, and in a friendly way, "Loukas the Joker."

EIGHT

The Tools Down the Well

One day when we were working at the marble yard—four craftsmen, myself and another apprentice—some news came which worried us. Returning from the neighbourhood tap where he had gone to fetch water, the other apprentice announced that the police were raiding all the workshops checking work licences, and those who didn't have one were being carted off to the police station. None of us Greeks working in the shop had such a licence. The three craftsmen were terrified and left immediately, taking with them the lad who had brought the news. There remained only Barba-Andrikos, who stood in for the boss when he was away, and me.

"You should leave as well, Stavri," the old man said to me anxiously.

"Why should I?" I replied, "What can they do to me? I'm not going anywhere. I won't leave you on your own."

Barba-Andrikos was terrified, though he did his best to

make it seem that he wasn't. At that moment two fierce-looking coppers arrived. It seems they'd spotted the others leaving. They asked the old man abruptly, as if they knew the situation at the workshop, "Where are the other craftsmen?"

Barba-Andrikos couldn't speak Turkish and when he tried to answer them, something like the noises a dumb person makes came out.

"What other craftsmen?" I asked in Turkish, "Can't you see that we're alone here?"

"Stop that talk, you no-gooder," one of them said angrily, "and whose tools are lying here?" he asked, indicating with his foot the tools left scattered by the fugitives in their terrified haste to get away.

"They're mine," I said suddenly, "mine and the old man's. Can't you see we're working here?" I indicated to him the chisel and the heavy, round work-stone I held in my hands, "Our job calls us to work in many different places."

"Be careful," said the second cop, who appeared to be of higher rank, "don't play clever with me or you'll find yourself in trouble. I don't swallow that stuff." And, turning to the other he ordered, "Go and call Nouri to come here to gather up these tools and take them to the station."

"What are they saying, Stavri?" Barba-Andrikos whispered to me.

"Shut up, old man," I told him sharply.

I was thinking that if the tools were taken, the others

would be obliged to go to the police station to ask for them; and they would have to pay a fine for not having licences and might even end up in jail.

"What are you doing?" I shouted at the policeman who had remained, and approached him angrily, "Will you take our tools? Those are holy things for a craftsman. I won't let you touch them!"

"Get back you hooligan!" he shouted at me and bent over to pick up a small tool that lay in front of him.

Like a maniac I shouted, "I'd rather destroy them than let you touch them!"

I grabbed as many of the tools that I could, rushed to the well that was at the rear of the workshop and threw them in.

Barba-Andrikos lost it. I just heard him saying fearfully as he pulled at his cheeks, "Stavri, my child, what are you doing? You'll destroy us."

At first, the Turk was stunned. Then he shouted fearfully, "This guy's crazy. He should be locked up!"

I continued frantically gathering up the tools and hurling them into the well, bellowing wildly. The old man was frozen, his eyes filled with tears, and as he panted, his moustache wobbled up and down making him look ridiculous. When the other policeman came back, together with a gendarme, to get the tools, their leader, the Komiseris, was waiting by the gate and shouted at them, "Don't go near him! He's crazy! He's throwing the tools down the well. He's dangerous, insane!"

The policeman was taken aback at first, but soon

rebounded, twirling his moustache and shouting like a *kabadayı*—a tough guy: "I'll fix that young bastard and his so-called madness!"

And he started to approach me, swearing as he came. The Komiseris grabbed him by the arm and shouted, terrified, "Don't provoke him. He'll bash you over the head or in the face with one of those heavy tools. Can't you see he's foaming at the mouth?"

The policeman hesitated, as if controlling his rage. Then the gendarme Nouri intervened—he knew me well as we had drunk together several times—"The Komiser Effendi is right," he said, "that fellow is completely crazy. The whole neighbourhood knows it. He suddenly goes crazy, like an epileptic, and then he's really dangerous. It's better to leave him alone now. If we try to tackle him, we don't know how things will end up."

He gave a secret sign to me to behave, and tactfully guided the others towards the gate. There the second policeman turned, spat towards me and shouted scornfully, "I spit on you, you worthless nutter!"

As soon as they were gone, I stopped my antics; but most of the tools were now at the bottom of the well. Then I got a good look at Barba-Andrikos. His face was pale and his eyes empty. I went towards him smiling and took his hand.

"Andriko," I said caressingly, "what's up with you?"

He looked at me closely, as if he wasn't sure who I was, and stuttered through trembling lips, "You're all right? There's nothing wrong with you?"

I made a head gesture to indicate no and chuckled.

The old man regained his courage and continued, "What can we do now, Stavraki? The tools..."

I didn't let him finish—"Is that what's worrying you? I'll go down the well and get them out. Calm down, we haven't suffered any loss. Aren't you glad we've escaped the fines, maybe even the lockup? The inspectors were so scared that they didn't even check us." But the old man looked at me again, terrified and sad, as if still afraid that I'd lost my mind.

At that moment the runaway craftsmen and their apprentice cautiously returned. They asked how we had managed to remain there and weren't in the lockup. Barba-Andrikos neither looked at them, nor said a word, and I kept quiet. They went to resume work, but apart from two or three scattered items, they couldn't find their tools. They asked Barba-Andrikos, but he avoided answering and looked at me fearfully.

"Your tools are at the bottom of the well," I told them suddenly and loudly, "I threw them there so the Turks wouldn't take them."

They were dumbstruck and looked uneasily at Barba-Andrikos, at me, at each other, and finally at the well, shouting "What are we going to do now, you idiot? How can we work without tools? How can we earn our wages and our children's bread?!"

Then they turned on Barba-Andrikos and shouted at

him almost threateningly, "And you, old man, why did you let the rascal do it?!"

I didn't let them continue and shouted over them, "Should I have let them take your tools so you would have had to pay a fine and end up in the lockup? You're like a bunch of ungrateful women. Stop whining, I'll get your tools out..."

"With a hook like catching a bonito fish?" said the apprentice in a high voice, sticking his face in everything.

"You'll lower me down the well and I'll dive down and get them," I said drily.

"What are you saying, Stavri?!" shouted old Andrikos, terrified.

"What will you use to get down there?" the others asked, both curious and frightened.

"Any rope we've got; the chains from the pulley, and if that's not enough, we'll tie your belts together. Let's go!"

But nobody moved; maybe the poor devils were scared that the rope would break, that I'd fall in and be drowned to death. In the meantime, Barba-Andrikos sent for the other apprentice to run to the house of the boss, who lived nearby, to tell him to get to the yard as soon as possible to forestall any disaster.

When I saw their fear, I pretended to reconsider, "If that's the way it is," I said, "and you won't help me. I'll go down on my own and get the tools out." Adding as if desperate, "What will be, will be." And I strode towards the well.

Barba-Andrikos almost screamed, "No, Stavri, my

child, stop...!" And instead of running towards me, he rushed to the gate to see if the boss was coming. The others didn't say a word and ran like automatons towards me. But I had already reached the well's mouth and had disappeared from their view. I heard them shouting, "Stavri! Stop! No, Stavri, no!"

At that moment, the boss, Mastro-Paschalis and his wife, ran in anxiously along with the apprentice, his neck extended and his eyes bulging in his eagerness to see what was going on. Paschalis, without waiting for any explanation from Barba-Andrikos, who was too upset to speak, asked the other three: "What's wrong with you? Why are you screaming like idiots?" Before they could explain to him, because they too were speechless with terror, I began hurling the tools out of the well, and soon emerged myself. As soon as Paschalis saw me approaching him in a comically triumphant manner, he burst out, laughing helplessly: "Man, you're completely crazy! And you've been working here all this time!"

The three craftsmen and Barba-Andrikos were still dumb-struck, as though they'd witnessed some sort of miracle. Madame Calypso asked her husband what was going on, and then began laughing uncontrollably too. The other apprentice crept up to the well and bent over to look in. I gave him a clout and he drew back terrified, calling on the Holy Virgin for aid.

The boss, still laughing, slapped me on the back: "You managed it again you son of Tatavla!" Then he turned to the old man, "And you my poor Andriko, didn't you know that the well is shallow? Did you think your favourite one was going to drown?”

In fact, the well wasn’t deep at all. It had slowly filled up from the pieces of marble and marble dust that we sometimes threw down there. It was only a little deeper than the height of a tall man and the water only came up to the knees; however Paschalis was the only one who had noticed this. I knew it too and this is the reason why:

Once, when I was alone at the yard, I noticed a policeman who was searching for the shop. He had some papers in his hand and looked back and forth between them and the workshop. I recognised him because I’d had dealings with him in the past over other matters. I was sure he was looking for me. At the time, I was mixed up in some erotic rivalries that were taking place at Kemer-Altı in Galata at some “House of Tolerance”—a bordello. I watched him from behind a pile of marble at the rear of the workshop and as soon as I saw him enter the yard, without giving much thought to what I was doing, I ran to the well, climbed over the rim, and with hands and feet clung-on to the ridges of the stones inside. If I’d remained behind the marble, he surely would have found me. I could only just hold-on by spreading my legs wide and clinging hard with my fingers. My heart was beating so wildly that it seemed to jolt my whole body, and I was scared that some earth and stones that were being dislodged would carry me down with them into the darkness and chaos. But I calmed down and tried to anchor myself more firmly, with my mind on the policeman. He had entered the yard and shouted loudly: "Hey, Stonemasons! Isn't anybody here?" He repeated himself three or four times and advanced into the yard, looking behind three or four stacks of marble and shouting angrily: "Hey, Masons!"

At that moment, the stones that were supporting my feet came loose and I suddenly slipped. My hands lost their grip and I felt myself falling straight down like a lead weight. I was terrified by the thought that I was going to be swallowed up in the depths of the earth, but I didn't cry out; it was as if I had accepted that I was done for. I could see myself dead, down there at the bottom of the well, covered by water. But before I had time to realise what was happening, I was suddenly jolted as if I had fallen from a low height, and without being dragged and bumped against the walls of the well. There was a splashing of water and I was wet up to my knees. The well was shallow. I gave a nervous laugh and felt myself hot at one moment, as with a fever, and the next freezing cold. I muffled a laugh, and tears of joy came to my eyes at the thought that I would get out of the hole in one piece and return to the people and places I loved.

At that moment, I heard the copper asking something, and the voice of Yakoumis the Naxiot answered angrily:

"The crazy kid must have gone and left the workshop empty and open again!" and to get rid of the copper, he added: "Mark my words, my Bey, I'll send him round to you myself when he gets back."

After a few moments, I climbed back up and stuck my head over the mouth of the well to see what was going on. Fortunately, the policeman had left. I jumped out of the well and ran to dust myself off and change my trousers. When Yakoumis saw me he was taken aback, "Where were you? That copper was looking for you and he certainly didn't want to kiss you. What are you doing, you nutcase, getting mixed up with the law again?"

"I was here," I answered carelessly, "I was in the rear washing my feet in the barrel. I didn't hear a thing."

I didn't say a word about the well and kept it to myself as a secret hideout.

So, when I came out of the well with the tools, the craftsmen rushed towards me laughing: "You saved us Stavri. Long may you live! May God reward you!"

"Go on, get the rest of the tools out yourselves," I replied, and went to clean myself up. But Barba-Andrikos held me and embraced me as if I had returned to life from a certain death. He didn't say a word, just looked at me with tears of joy in his eyes. The old man loved me in his own way. Always calling me, "My child," and showing me tirelessly how to tackle the work. To him I owe most of what I learned. May his days be happy.

Paschalis shook his head and looked at me smiling. Madame Calypso, too, was smiling: "May good befall you, Stavri," she said, "I haven't laughed like that since I saw Mr Punch!"

. . .

From then on, every time the police came to check the licences, the craftsmen threw their tools down the well and sat with arms crossed. They told the officers that they had been out of work for some time and were waiting for the Boss to give them work, so they could feed their children; and that if they got work, they would come straight round to the police station to pay for their licences, since they were honest men and respected the land that gave them bread. The inspectors wished them well and went on their way, happy to have carried out their duty, with me serving as their dragoman.

NINE

Mehmet the Mason, Round as a Cannon-Ball

At Paschali Tiniakos's Marble Works of Phedias at Fındıklı worked a Turk who was short and fat; a rounded face, body and arms, and legs which resembled fat sausages. His name was Mehmet, but the other workers and I—four Greeks, a Levantine and a Maltese—called him "Taşçı-Topuz Mehmet," which means "Stoneworker Mehmet Round as a Cannon-Ball." He came from a village near Kayseri and wore the local costume: a short black-felt salvar with gaiters, a heavy blue-woollen shirt and over it a dark aubergine-coloured waistcoat with sleeves. Around his waist was a wide yellow and white cummerbund of coarse wool and on his feet, thick, white-woollen socks and Yemeni style slippers with iron at the heels and round nails all over the soles. His big, bushy eyebrows met over a flat nose, his cheeks were pink, and a thick moustache fell over his lips. However, when he looked at you his chestnut eyes were lit with such kindness that they seemed to caress you.

He was never without his low fez, which was bound by a turban-like green kerchief and nestled on the back of his head, just above a thick roll of flesh which resembled a sausage round his neck. The green turban indicated that he had been a member of some sacred order since childhood. For that reason, he was very religious and said his prayers regularly. Over all his other thick woollen garments he had tied a piece of short-haired, curly-black rams wool material, which hung down his back like a saddle and was tied in front under his rounded belly. When he performed his prayers, he spread this on the ground and knelt on it, having first washed his hands, feet and head in a barrel. This took place behind a large heap of marble. Immediately afterwards he would return to his work.

He sat on the ground, took the block between his legs and began the heavy chipping. His belly and hips shook over the stone and you'd think he was going to crush it. Every so often he would wipe his hand over the area he was chipping and touch it as if he were trying to feel the marble's heartbeat. He did all his work faster than the rest of us because he was a skilful and conscientious craftsman. As soon as he had finished, while his sweat was still wetting the stone, he would say in a simple voice: "Mastor bitti — Boss, I've finished," and Paschalis would set him another task.

At first, we used to tease him mercilessly, but kindly Topuz Mehmet soon chastened us. One time we put nails in his prayer mat and when he knelt to pray, they stuck into him. He didn't get angry, just removed them patiently one by one and put them into his waistcoat, murmuring, as if to someone, "Well look, I didn't own any of these little things..."

Another time we pretended we were arguing with the Levantine and the Maltese and laughing shamelessly, contrived to spill a large container of water over his head. Topuz Mehmet didn't say a word. He got up slowly and began to shake the water from his clothes. His heavy and clumsy movements reminded us of a dancing bear. We burst out laughing, and clapping our hands, began the bear song: "Oyna Mehmet, oyna Mehmet — Dance, Mehmet, dance."

Mehmet didn't get angry. He continued shaking the water off his clothes, then stopped, raised his hands and eyes to heaven and said quietly: "May God reward you. You've cooled me down."

We were stunned. The laughter froze on our lips. The teasing words choked in our mouths. Suddenly we saw Topuz Mehmet with other eyes, like a saint full of kindness whom we had been tyrannising. We looked from one to another as if criticising each other without being able to speak, our throats choked with bitterness.

So he reacted to all our teasing with "Çocuklar, canım — They are just children." No swearing, no slurs, nothing.

He usually kept his eyes lowered, and when he did raise them, he looked around, breathed deeply and whispered:

"Şükür Allah – Thanks be to God." Whatever he saw around him, he gazed at with a restrained wonder, and his face would slowly take on an expression of bliss. This made an impression on me and I wanted to learn the reason.

"My child," he said, "a man mustn't forget that he belongs to the earth in which he lives. But above all, there is God, above everything our eyes behold; all the beautiful things he gave us to see and for our souls to enjoy."

When he ate, he opened and spread out a large cherry-coloured handkerchief from his village in which his food was wrapped: bread, onions or garlic, olives and halva made from sesame. As he ate, he made sure that nothing fell outside his tablecloth, and when he had finished, he gathered every last crumb and placed them in a corner to be eaten by the insects, which he said were God's creatures too. Every time he belched, he gave thanks to God, and one day I asked him:

"What has God got to do with it?"

"My child, my stomach digests well, I am thanking God for keeping me strong so that I can enjoy my food."

And so, day by day, as if we were imbued with his Anatolian wisdom, not only did we stop teasing him, but we helped him in his work as far as we were able. Topuz Mehmet was moved by this. He bought soft roasted chickpeas from a fellow villager and offered them to us. When that man came to the yard to visit him, the two of them withdrew behind a heap of unworked marble. There they perched opposite each other like two birds. After exchanging greetings, they became silent and gazed into each other's eyes, as though they saw mirrored there their great pain and longing for their far away homeland. Then they began to speak quietly:

"The plane trees by the mosque will be in bloom now... the birds will have returned by now and are singing...the Hoca will be sitting by the spring and the children will be playing by the water in the sunshine..."

And each one opened his eyes wide as though seeing a vision. Then they continued looking into each other's eyes as if conversing with their glances. After a while, one of them added:

"If it has rained a lot the corn will be ripening sweetly. The woods will be full of flowers and the deer running freely with their young..." and again, they fell into their peaceful daydream until Topuz Mehmet said, "Fatma will have had another child. How many other girls, I wonder, will be expecting," and the other continued, with sadness in his voice: "And poor Ayşe will still be waiting..."

They were silent again and gazed at each other like two innocent creatures silently sharing their sadness and joy until they rose as if unburdened, saying "Allah Kerim — With God's help." They took each other's hands and after a mutual "Güle-güle — Farewell," the chickpea seller placed his portable table and wares over his shoulder, stuck his bronze scales in his cummerbund, picked up his sieve, which looked like a small tambourine, and left. Topuz Mehmet returned to his work, his eyes still filled with a melancholy daydream. These visits, and the way these two simple people passed their time, made me respect and love Topuz Mehmet even more and caused me to realise the worth of silence between two male friends with mutual feelings.

Topuz Mehmet lived in a *han*, as large as a caravansary, far away on the outskirts of the old "Turkish City," as the Greeks called it, by the walls of Byzantium. He slept piled into a room with several people from his village. At the time of the Massacres of the Armenians he didn't take part, even though the marble yard was temporarily closed. However, innocent as he was, he believed some Levantine "important people" when they told him that they had lost the keys to their bank vaults and had to save some important heirlooms. During the chaos of the time, they got him to open a hole in the wall of a light-well in the bank's basement from which their cracksmen entered and carried out their work. Who knows how much they took in gold, jewels and title deeds. As payment Topuz Mehmet took no more than a day's wages with a little tip on top; and he came and divided that among the lads at the marble yard because he had borrowed tools from there to do the job. He'd been recommended by our Levantine co-worker, who was well rewarded by the members of his gang.

At the time of the Great Cholera of Constantinople, Topuz Mehmet didn't turn up at the yard one day; neither the next, nor the following days. He came no more. We became uneasy. When one of us wasn't there, something was missing from the yard. We spoke about him more than our other acquaintances and friends who we knew were ill. I was overcome with anxiety until the day came when I couldn't control myself any longer and I set out to find my friend Topuz Mehmet, to see if he was alive, to save him.

After wandering through unknown parts of the Boundless City, I came upon the *han* where he lived; but two big guys who were standing guard at the yard gate wouldn't let me in. They had put ropes around the building because many of the country Turks who were piled in there had the cholera and were dying one after the other. The road, the walls of the *han* and the guards' feet were covered in lime-wash.

I circled the building looking for another entrance or window to enter. There was nothing there, not even a hole. Everywhere bare walls and only high up, under the eaves, a row of small barred windows like a prison. I made my way back to the entrance and as soon as I got there saw someone showing the guards a paper which allowed him to enter. I hid against the corner of a wall and with a pencil scrawled some unreadable letters on a piece of paper. I could speak Turkish, but didn't know how to write it, but I was sure the guards were illiterate too. I covered my shoes with lime-wash, mustered my courage and approached the gate.

But at that moment a cart came out through the grand arch of the yard. It was filled to the brim with lime as if heading for a building site. The carter, who was pulling the horse, and another man who followed him with a spade over his shoulder like a weapon, were wearing strange clothing, something like loose nightgowns of rough sacking, with caps of the same material and wide leather leggings. Everything was smeared with lime. These costumes made their appearance both comic and terrifying. Suddenly, the bumping of the cart over the rough cobblestones caused blackened, skeletal human-limbs to appear from the lime: legs, arms and a head which you'd have said was gasping for air.

I couldn't believe my eyes and trembled with fear. The gate appeared to me like a huge mouth that spewed forth the dead so as to swallow the living—the soldiers and I—who had moved back from the entrance. My first thought was to leave, but then in my mind's eye I saw Topuz Mehmet in agony under such a macabre heap. I went forward and showed my paper to one of the soldiers. Without bothering to examine it, he made a gesture for me to pass.

As soon as I entered, I stopped, dazed, and looked around me. The building was a huge, old, three-storied *han* with a series of open arches on each floor. Its three sides surrounded a stone-paved yard, in the middle of which was a huge, dilapidated fountain with many taps from which one or two were hissing with water. The entrance side was enclosed by an enormous wall, thick like that of a castle, with only one arched door. The yard was heavily whitened with lime-wash, and in front of the stairs and on every side of the *han* was lime dust piled high as if to obstruct Death from leaving or entering.

. . .

From one stair, two men dressed like those I had seen earlier were bringing down skeletal, half-naked corpses, their faces distorted by suffering and the agony of death. A turbid, foul-smelling liquid fell from them, polluting the air. The two gatherers of the dead, with their hands bound with lime-soaked linen, took the bodies by the legs and arms and threw them onto a cart, one above the other. When they had filled it, they covered it with lime, hitting with their spades anything that protruded; arms, legs and heads. By the opposite stair two other workmen were piling bodies beside the lime. I watched terrified, scared that I would recognise Topuz Mehmet amongst the pile of bodies. I trembled with grief and it seemed as though I heard deep groans coming from those horrible corpses and that hands and legs were slowly moving, as if to grab hold of something and be saved.

I lifted my eyes and looked along the arches hoping I'd see Topuz Mehmet gesturing for me to come and save him. But the open arches seemed to look back at me like the empty eye-sockets of skulls. I didn't know what to do, where to go, where to start. I couldn't think clearly. Then I saw the man who had entered before me. He came and gave orders to those who were piling the bodies. I ran to him and asked him if he knew "Kayserili Mehmet — Mehmet from Kayseri," the stone worker. After telling me that he was a health worker, he asked what I was doing there as it was a dangerous and forbidden place and told me that I must leave at once. But then, seeing the agony on my face, he added more gently that the stronger had been moved elsewhere and only the cholera-stricken and dying remained. He finished by saying "Good luck. Don't touch anything. You're lost if you do."

In despair I went up to the third stair, which seemed empty. I held my handkerchief over my face as the stench was sickening. I reached the first floor. The arches formed corridors with a series of cell-like rooms. I didn't meet a living soul; only two dead, one lying face down on the floor, the other grasping the stone bench in a room as if he wanted to rise and shout. From half-open doors I sometimes heard stifled gasping for breath and in doorways there were pools of dirty liquid which gave off an unbearable stench of death that penetrated guts and brain. I bunched the ends of my handkerchief and stuffed them up my nostrils, while I held the rest of it over my lips. I could only just breathe. But every now and again I was obliged to remove it and shout in despair:

"Topuz Mehmet...azizim...neredesin? — Where are you?"

Ready to cry, I kicked open doors and looked desperately within; but on the first floor Topuz Mehmet was nowhere to be found. I stood before the stair to the second floor disheartened, breathless and overcome with nausea. The sweat poured off my brow and my legs felt weak. Should I leave or should I continue? There was no hope, but Topuz Mehmet was waiting for me; I could see him in my mind's eye.

I gritted my teeth and went up the stair as fast as I could to gain time; for him and for me. On the top stair of the second flight, the body of another victim was spread face-down, his eyes open, fixed on the stairway he hadn't managed to descend. Again, I began kicking open the doors, and opening the third one it seemed to me that I came face to face with Topuz Mehmet. I recognised him; skeletal, right there in the corner of the cell, my friend, Stoneworker Mehmet. A human carcass without flesh, half-naked; only bones covered with blackened skin and around him that dirty liquid; you'd think he'd thrown off his flesh and it was rotting. His face was lost amongst his eyebrows and moustache. His eyes were sunken and closed. He still wore his fez and turban. I went over to him, leaned over and shouted, my eyes full of tears from sadness and nausea.

"Topuz Mehmet — Azizim!"

And at that moment Mehmet half-opened his eyes. He looked at me. It seemed to me that he tried to raise his right hand; his glance slightly brightened, smiling faintly. I think I heard him whisper breathlessly: "Ogloum — My son."

I stretched out my hand: "Baba — Father."

But it was too late. Topuz Mehmet turned his head and looked at me, his eyes wide, dim, but full of kindness.

I was overcome by an unbearable grief mixed with awe.

So I left without seeing clearly through my tear-filled eyes Stonemason Topuz Mehmet, dead before me, but alive within my heart.

TEN

Hadji Minas's Hash-Den

Between Yeni Şehir and Dolapdere, a little further-on than the great slope of Feridiye Djaddesi was a hash-den; the "Teke of Hadji Minas" by name, a secret name. It lay somewhere in a crooked alleyway between those two shabby neighbourhoods which were populated by workers and the poor, most of them Greek. An out of the way retreat in a quiet area; and, if you did not know the way, you could easily lose yourself trying to find it in a labyrinth of twisting, narrow alleys—just the right spot for a *teke*. You wouldn't have thought that not very far from a main street like Feridiye Avenue, where respectable Greeks and other races lived, there would be such a *lokal*, such a hang-out.

There, among the yards and small houses of the lane with its broken cobbles in a low building which didn't attract your eye was the *teke*. Two steps led up to the front gate. Three windows on the left and a smaller one on the right—all with wooden shutters painted blue—made up the façade, which resembled the other low houses and small shops of the neighbourhood. The gate gave onto a small, square front yard without a roof, only a pergola covered by a rose bush and a wisteria. On the right side of the yard a glass door opened into a little room that contained the smaller window facing the road. Here, one or two of the young hash-smokers who were attached to old Hadji Minas as bodyguards slept. From there a curtained doorway led to a corridor off which were the toilet and a wash basin, and finally, to a secret door which gave onto the rear yard of the *teke*. The side of the front yard facing the main entrance was covered by a glass wall made up of coloured opaque panes which resembled those of a church or mosque. These lit the front yard pleasantly, but prevented you seeing what was happening in the main yard behind. Several wooden benches ran along the yard walls on either side of the doors and faced the glass wall. On the side to the left of the gate, a double door led into the *sala* of the *teke*.

The *sala* was a long, narrow room. From end to end of the two long sides were divans with coverings and soft cushions made from cherry-coloured kilims. In front of them was set out a row of round tables of dark, chestnut wood. Around each one, on the side opposite the divan, three low, wide chairs with backs and rests for one arm were placed in a half-circle. They were painted green, with seats of woven soft rushes which glistened faintly with wear. On each table was a form of bronze lighter, something like a censer, with a thin layer of embers under ashes and a small pair of tongs to light cigarettes and pipes. The floor was of marble tiles spread with thick, straw matting which swallowed up the sound of footsteps. On the lime-washed, rose-coloured walls hung coloured lithographs in ornate, golden frames. There were portraits of beautiful women, blondes and brunettes, exotic birds, sea-views with ships, hunting scenes with wild beasts, forests with flowing streams, castles in the mountains, lakes with boats and lit-up palaces; a world of colour to bewitch both children and adults with child-like souls.

On the blue-painted, wooden ceiling, narrow white strips formed a network from which hung various strange objects, some from strings, others from wires, some high up, others so low they could be touched by stretching your arm and standing on tiptoe. Glass golden-coloured balls reflected your face, normally from one viewpoint comically distorted from another. Necklaces of brightly coloured beads had charms at their ends: "The Hand of Fatma," which protects, and "The Blue Eye," which wards off evil. From large bobbins hung threads like loosened hair, black, blonde, auburn. Ribbons of silk and shining paper swayed like snakes. Amidst it all appeared starfish, huge crabs black as spiders which wove invisible nets, red lobsters with long antennae and huge claws, along with small shells with iridescent mother-of-pearl like jewels. Unusual objects were supposed to bring good luck: the jawbone of a horse whitened by the waves and decorated with birds, spiral golden ram's horns, scarlet painted horseshoes with gold nails. Amidst it all, children's toys: figures from the Karagöz shadow play with cymbals on their arms and legs, puppets that moved their limbs as if unhinged, little rosy-skinned blond angels, dolls with white bridal veils—their arms open as if for an embrace—and near them some oarsmen with their caiques, ready, you'd say, to steal them away. Various animals: dogs, cats, sheep, donkeys, frogs, butterflies made from coloured celluloid which moved as if playing, large and small sheep's bells, goat's bells, which sounded so you'd think that the animals were wearing them.

There was no absence of plants and flowers: maize with its tufts hanging down like beards and the leaves open like the hats of clowns, wheat stalks woven together like fans, strings of quinces, pomegranates, apples, lemons, oranges which perfumed the air along with flowers: carnations, jasmine, roses, and violets which the Hadji cut fresh from his garden and hung in glass vases like candles in the mosque. Aromatic herbs: basil, mint, marjoram and rosemary planted in pots and placed next to gaudy paper flowers which seemed to give off sweet smells too.

Also scattered across the ceiling were glass lanterns of various colours. Elsewhere cages hung, with two or three songbirds in each: greenfinches, linnets, goldfinches, sky larks. One cage hung slightly lower than the others, it was made of golden wire decorated with blue beads to keep away the evil-eye and contained a white and yellow canary. The old Hadji, who loved it particularly, would stand on tip-toe to speak to it nose-to-nose and to place on its tongue a special food which made it sing, as he said, better than the most famous prima donnas in the world—which for him meant The City.

Among this unbelievable world of floating objects of every shape and colour there were also five ships, spaced apart from each other: frigates and three-masted galleons completely outfitted; with their sails open, they were ready to set sail between heaven and earth across the mid-air sea of a world that was both imaginary and real.

From the four corners of the ceiling, chains made of wide links of coloured paper met in the centre at its *omphalos*, as if protecting that exotic canopy. From the *omphalos* hung the only kerosene lamp, large with a double wick, casting its green-blue light over the pictures and lower walls while leaving the ceiling and its universe in the half-light. In winter the *teke* was warmed by two large, gleaming, copper braziers placed at either end of the *sala*. In one corner hung the *çalgı*—the musical instruments—a tambourine and a bouzouki.

At the far end of the *sala* was another smaller room that was entered through a low wooden door with a small rose-shaped hole in it at the height of a man's eye. This "rear shop" was illuminated through a glass door which gave onto the back yard; this was paved with marble tiles, the joins between which were regularly white-washed by Minas as was the habit of his forebears who came from the "Orthodox island of Syra," as he said, although he was born in the neighbourhood of Fasoulas in Smyrna. Beside this rear room, but without direct access from it, was a storeroom for food and household utensils, and on the floor above was the Hadji's kitchen, which was reached by a narrow ladder and through a hatch. The other rooms of his dwelling were laid out in an L-shape on the south side of the rear yard and enjoyed abundant light. At the west side of them a stairway, like those on a ship, led up to a *hayati*, an enclosed gallery, which jutted out over the yard. From there one entered the lodgings of the elderly Minas, where his wife and daughter lived unseen by strangers' eyes, their privacy guarded by the abundance of sweet-smelling herbs and flowers in pots which—tended by those two hard-working and tidy women—flooded the gallery and transformed it into a hanging garden.

A jasmine plant, with a thin, strong trunk, rose up from the yard and spread over the whole roof of the *hayati*, falling forwards over its front to form a fragrant latticework which hid the interior from any curious glance. A honeysuckle, equally old, and in bloom, climbed up a lattice frame-work as far as the gallery roof where it joined its sweet-smelling yellow flowers with the white blooms of the jasmine. This honeysuckle, with its long shoots and thick foliage hid the Hadji's yard from the eyes of his neighbours. By mounting the gallery staircase to a certain point you could part the branches and enter the neighbour's yard and from its gate slip into the narrow alleyways without being seen. The neighbour allowed this without complaint thanks to the generosity of Hadji

Minas, who thus ensured, in the case of any "emergency," a way out for his clients. To the right of the honeysuckle, in a low cellar at the corner of the yard, piles of wood and charcoal were stored. From this cellar a small wooden door gave way onto a narrow lane, where one's traces would soon be lost among the meandering alleyways. This exit was used by the women of the house so they would not have to pass through the front yard of the *teke*. In another corner of the yard, a chicken–run housed the domestic animals which completed Hadji Minas's "household": an Angora goat with a long silver coat from which it took its name, "Asimi." Four fat, dappled hens, the "*sultanes*," formed the harem of a tall well-built cock, whose feathers were black and shone like steel, while his scarlet, martial looking comb swayed rhythmically from side to side as he strutted up and down like a general on parade. He sounded the hours, and every now and then rode one of the *sultanes*—insatiably like a satyr—crowing afterwards to announce his erotic triumph while the lady shook herself to tidy up her dress which had been knocked out of shape by the force of the coming together.

This cock was the Old Man's pride and joy. He admired it for being so good at doing what he could no longer do and was proud of his "*mangas*," as he affectionately called it. He took it to Cock-Fights where he pitted it against other fighting-cocks and trained it continuously for these contests. He had given it the fighting-name "Kahraman," Turkish for "hero," and it was a true hero as it almost always won those bloody battles.

The Old Man celebrated its victories as though they were his own, along with his closest friends. The table would be decorated with vases containing not flowers, but the feathers of the defeated cocks tied into bunches and labelled with their names, the names of their owners, where they were from and the date and place of the combat. After the meal, Minas would store the feathers in a jewel-box inside a large wooden trunk. In a smaller, more beautiful box he preserved like holy relics the few feathers that Kahraman had lost in battle.

Roaming freely in the yard was Yabandji, a mongrel sheep-dog with white hair that looked as though it had been badly trimmed and red eyes like those of an albino. It was so clever that the Hadji's friends said that if it could talk, it would out smart any human. Yabandji was an uninvited guest who had finally been accepted by the Old Minas thanks to its disarming persistence and engaging cheekiness. Whenever he threw it out, it left like some unfortunate soul with its tail between its legs, only to return shortly afterwards bouncing joyfully. In time it picked up its master's disgust for people wearing uniform, barking fiercely at their legs. Indeed, it had the gift of sensing when such a person was passing down the alleyway and would start howling as if some great disaster had befallen the world, while the growling continued until long after the enemy had gone.

Two more pets completed the Hadji's four-legged crew: Psipsina, dressed in grey, and Niarniaris, with a black suit and pure white shirt-front—two cats, mother and son. The latter regularly impregnated the former, scandalising the innocent hash-smokers and the Old Man, who saw in this action "The finger of the Goddess Providence." The Stars were seven pure white doves who flew around freely all day, flirting or pairing off and cooing their passion, and at night nested under the *hayati*. But the Old Man's greatest and rarest treasure was The Rainbow, a peacock, beautiful and stately, which strutted with ritual-like steps around the yard all day, sometimes with its feathers closed, sometimes triumphantly open, offering the Old Man's wife and daughter a spectacle of which they never tired. Minas worshipped it like an idol and gave it special attention. At night he didn't put it into the chicken-run; in summer it slept in the cool of the *hayati* and in winter in the warmth of the house. He would take it up the stairs cradled tenderly in his embrace, or encourage it to go up alone, slowly, step by step, dragging its tail behind like a potentate's robes.

The Old Hadji kept the chicken-run spotlessly clean, and in front of it was an acacia with sweet-smelling golden yellow blooms, while on either side two, old vines formed a shady covering with their leaves and branches from which hung bunches of grapes. Hadji Minas ear-marked the amber fruit from one vine for his household and for his closest friends to occasionally sweeten their mouths. From the abundant small, black grapes of the other he made a red wine that slipped down the throat like a sweet flame and scented the mouth, awakening and stimulating the nervous system. From the stalks and leavings from both vines he made a small amount of tsipouro that would "make the paralysed walk," as he said. Although they respected the Old Man and his kindness, the children of the neighbourhood would climb over the wall and up the vine, eating the grapes and smearing their faces like little fauns. He sometimes let them get away with this, as it reminded him of the escapades of his own childhood.

Under the vines, against one of the high outer walls, was the marble relief of a dolphin from whose mouth water flowed into a large trough. To the right and left of this, low seats were built against the wall. In a flowerbed in the centre of the yard an abundance of large poppies grew. From these Minas drew the amount of opium that was required for the special preparation of the hashish. All around the yard, in other flowerbeds, in large and small pots, on the ground, on shelves—even hanging—bloomed an abundance of beautiful and aromatic flowers which the Hadji used to decorate the *sala* of the *teke*.

At times when there was no work Hadji Minas would gather a few of his closest friends under the cool shade of the vine, next to the lulling murmur of the fountain, to enjoy together the tranquillity of silent reflection, with the eyes open in that little Eden. In that forgotten corner they exchanged the delights of hashish for the enjoyment of the opium which the Old Man smoked unadulterated, offering it discretely in turn to the others. Sometimes he offered them his wine, or fiery tsipouro, to drink in sips, as when taking communion. This was exceptional to the habits of the *teke*, where alcohol was forbidden. These privileged *arkadaşlar*, or friends, greatly appreciated the enjoyment of the opium and the drinks, and even more the behaviour of the Hadji and the preference he showed them, and so became strongly attached to their "Hadji-Baba."

In one corner of the "rear shop" was the *odjak*—a hearth, where there were always glowing embers and hot ashes. On this, to one side, was a large bronze *ibrik*—a vessel with a long handle, which gleamed from constant rubbing, always full of fresh water. It was here that the Hadji prepared the hashish and readied the pipes and *nargiles*. The coffee was made in the corner opposite the *odjak* on a gypsy-style round brazier, which was set into the wall with a large hole in the ceiling directly over it so the smell of coffee would escape and not become mixed with the aroma of the hashish and spoil it. Also, on the brazier was a green porcelain Chinese teapot full of Persian tea. This was very heavy and was kept well covered to prevent the aroma of its steam from escaping. For each customer, Minas diluted a little of this tea with scalding water and served it steaming hot and sweet-smelling. On shelves between the *odjak* and the brazier were coffee cups, gold-decorated Persian tea-glasses, water glasses, two or three red clay jars full of sweets, mastic and rose petals, as well as several carafes of different sherbets: cherry, orange, orgeat, mint—all prepared by the spotlessly clean hands of Minas's wife. The "tools" of the *teke*, however, were nowhere to be seen. Neither those used to prepare the hashish nor the pipes.

No one could suspect where the first were hidden away; the second, Hadji Minas presented at the appropriate moment, like a conjurer.

The small, bare space of the "rear shop" was always ready to face a police raid as it resembled an ordinary "Café-Odjak" where the "Usta" prepared the coffees, teas, *nargiles* and sherbets. In fact it was the Holy of Holies of the ritual of hashish. All types came here to smoke dope: novices, those who had smoked a few times, dedicated smokers and addicts. None of them could do without Hadji Minas who had his own way of doing everything: preparing the hashish and pipes, initiating the newcomers and giving pleasure to the *meraklides*—the devotees. These rituals took place in an environment completely unlike that of any other *teke* and in that phantasmagorical setting, that deceptive paradise offered to them by the Old Hadji, the customers were exalted to a higher level of enjoyment, which is why the *teke* was famed among a limited number of fanatically loyal connoisseurs.

Hadji Minas prepared the hashish with his own hands. From a friend in the Mısır Çarşı—an old Tatar with a pure and white patriarchal beard—he bought the choicest golden yellow Indian cannabis powder, packed in silk bags so tightly woven they seemed like chamois leather. From this powder he prepared two types of hashish. He weighed-up an amount by eye, placed it in a silver dish and browned it over a low flame, stirring it slowly with a twig from an evergreen bush; two materials which ensured that the aroma and essence of the hashish remained unaltered.

When the yellow powder began to change colour he sprinkled it lightly with pure opium and musk, which gave a pleasing taste; this was the *karışık*—the "mixed" hashish, one of his specialities. The other type, which contained only unadulterated hashish, was the *sade*—the "pure" hashish. As the browning proceeded, the dust began to darken and give-off a smell, pleasant at first but becoming heavy, and the mixture produced a thick oil which with mixing stiffened the powder until it became a dark brown paste. Minas then removed the mixture from the heat, stirred it and allowed it to cool. After washing his hands carefully and drying them over the fire, he took hold of the paste and began to knead it with his fingers, smelling it from time to time. When he judged that it was ready, he used his fingers to cut it up and with his heated palms rolled it into sticks shaped like thick macaroni. He then cut what he intended to sell to his customers into cigarette-sized pieces. The greater part, which was for use in the *teke*, he rolled into snail-shaped chunks and hid them where nobody, not even his wife knew, and where nobody would discover them. However, he kept a few small bits for himself in a special pocket.

In the daytime the *teke* opened late, around midday, and then only for show. Between dawn and opening time Hadji Minas took his first short sleep, his night-sleep; during those hours the *teke* was completely quiet. A few elderly customers, along with some young men who couldn't manage without the Hadji, came to drink their midday coffee in silent company with the Old Man. It was enough for them to drink with him. In the afternoon everybody left and the *teke* was shut. Only a few young helpers remained to help the Hadji put everything in order: to prepare the place for the holy rituals of the night, clean up the garden and run errands for the household and the *teke*. The Old Man worked along with the young lads, but when he tired, around dusk, he would say, as if asking for permission, "May I go yavrumlar?" and went up to the house for his second short sleep, which was the afternoon one.

In the evening, as it grew dark, the shutters of the front gate and windows half-opened, like eyelids after sleep; and as soon as night fell the coming of the faithful began. They came one by one or two by two, serious and silent. You'd say they were weighed down by something they bore within them. When the weather was good, they sat for a while on the benches in the front yard enjoying the coolness and the aroma of the roses and wisteria. They spoke quietly and reflectively, measuring their words: Turks, Russians, Muslims, Christians, heterodox, they greeted each other warm-heartedly with a "Merhaba," a "Yeia sas," placing the right hand on the chest and bowing the head slightly. They then entered the *sala* unhurriedly and took whatever seat fell to them. You'd say they didn't want to disturb the calm which reigned within the *teke*. The social position of each of them interested neither the owner nor the habitués. The faithful at the Teke of Hadji Minas were all kinds of people: rich and poor, well-dressed and poorly dressed, men from the capital in

European clothes, and provincials in local costume. Men in high positions sat next to labourers, *daïdes* opposite humble householders, Government Officials and military men beside *kabadayı* and hardened criminals—but there, beside Old Hadji Minas and their other friends, all were humble; they became different people. Everyone was welcome in that warm and peaceful refuge. Old Minas with his presence, his strict kindness and his impartial judgement was respected by all and favoured no one whoever he might be. Among those intellectually disparate and socially opposed people he created brotherly intimacy and warm harmony, since they all respected the *teke* as a holy place and worshipped Hadji-Minas as a saintly figure who gifted them with blissful reveries.

When inside the *teke*, the faithful were like the members of some secret sect, equal in what they enjoyed and united in whatever took place there. Among them were a few fanatic addicts who from a surfeit of hashish had become unsuitable for any work which required physical effort; all they could manage was some coming and going and hanging about, or above all, sitting and daydreaming with eyes half-closed. The Hadji not only gave them free hashish, but also a little pocket-money; treatment which made them so dedicated to him that they would have sacrificed their lives. They formed his personal bodyguard and at the same time the "garrison" of the *teke*. They had sworn themselves to uncover any suspicious customers and to forestall any surprise raids by the police.

Every new initiate was accompanied by a regular and was greeted with a heart-felt "Hoş geldin — Welcome" by the Hadji. The bodyguards however, carefully watched the newcomer's every move to be sure he wasn't a spy and were ready to take any necessary measures. There was no chance of an unknown stranger being accepted, and guards were on the look-out at key points; one at each corner of the alley, another hung around casually outside the *teke*, a fourth sat in the front yard.

The front shutters were closed earlier than the time set by the police for shops to shut, as though it were a place without business. The façade of the *teke* was completely dark, but inside a different life had quietly begun in a warm and friendly atmosphere, without any uproar or shouting and with the participation of all the hash-smokers and their leader Hadji Minas. After the front gate had closed, latecomers would enter through the two back yard doors, where guards had already taken position. Old Minas knew all the faithful personally, their feelings, their talk, their individual ways. But when they were gathered in the *teke* there was no difference between them since one and all had the same longing: to smoke "the black." The Hadji greeted them warmly, "Maşallah! Maşallah!" as we might say "Glory be to God we are strong and healthy," and continued talking in a lively way which opened their hearts. To stimulate their desire, he delayed giving the order "Hacı doldur," in other words, "Hadji fill the pipes."

When the order was finally given it was not in a commanding way, but quietly and repeated by many like a request to the Old Man.

He entered the "holy of holies," along with two or three of his assistants who showed him everything they did and waited for his approval like young school children. If the Old Man saw them making any mistake, he immediately corrected it without humbling them. All his *nargiles* were made of walnut wood which years of use had made smooth and shiny like some unknown precious material, and after each was prepared they were lined up on the edge of the hearth to keep warm. When all were ready, Minas put a little charcoal on those to be smoked and tested each one to see if it was alright, while the youths watched him dedicatedly. Sometimes, much to their delight, he asked them to test the *nargiles* themselves. When this process was completed the Old Man blew into the pipe of one of the *nargiles*, as if into a flute, and produced high-pitched joyful notes. This was the invitation signal. At once the faithful, who had been waiting impatiently in the *sala*, entered the "holy of holies," one behind the other, silently as if in a church. The Hadji received them with a warm "Hoş geldiniz azizler – Welcome dear ones."

Within that simple and bare refuge, without even a stool, each one took the place that fell to his turn. Most remained upright, others squatted on their heels, some sat on the ground with their legs crossed, a few knelt. All mixed together without distinction. One would have said that the austere bareness of that small space communicated to the faithful the humility that one should feel during the performance of a rite.

The smoking began with the "mixed" hashish. With his thick thumb, Minas pressed into each *nargile* a bedding of pure Isfahan tobacco. On this he placed the "mixed" hashish with its traces of opium and musk, which he cut finely with his front teeth so it wouldn't lose any of its precious properties; finally, on top, went a few glowing charcoal embers. The number of "mixed" smokes was fixed by the Hadji according to the mood of the smokers. These *nargiles* were a pleasant prelude to an evening's smoking. The water in the pipes contained a little mint which gave off an open and cool aroma which combined well with the "mixed black" and gave it a particularly pleasant taste. After the "mixed" *nargiles*, the smoking continued until its end with doses, becoming slowly weaker, of the *sade*, prepared from unadulterated hashish with all its pure qualities. This permeated and slowly worked on the organism, the feelings, the minds, and souls of the smokers, eventually producing a euphoria which, if it didn't knock them out, led them to other worlds—the worlds they yearned for.

The Hadji decorated each *nargile* with a small garland of thin blue beads and a *hajmali*, a charm, which the smokers believed would protect them from the evil eye and allow them to fully enjoy their smoke. It was exactly these smoking implements, along with the equipment for the preparation of the hashish, that the authorities wished to uncover. But Hadji Minas, like an old fox, hid them where not even the finest undercover cops of the *devriye*, the patrols, could find them when from time to time—as a show of their zeal and authority—they decided to make sudden raids on suspicious *lokals* of that type. Hadji Minas didn't avoid these surprise intrusions, though with his connections it would have been possible for him to do so. His defences were well organised, and he was ready to confront his pursuers. He knew how to appease the "Upholders of the Law" with suitable friendly gifts, enough for him to close their mouths and eyes and for them to look on the "Hadji Baba"—as they called him—as a friend, even a benefactor. Among his customers, all of whom were devoted to him, were several with high posts in "The Machinery of the State" including, naturally, the police. By them, Minas was warned in good time of raids being planned by the *devriye* and was able to forestall any danger. The Hadji also knew which day the patrols would begin their operation as he had infiltrated one of his men among them. As soon as news of a raid reached his ears, the *teke* changed its appearance. The truth was that there was nothing suspicious about it to bring to mind the other *tekes* in The City. This was thanks to the innovative ideas that Minas—an artist of his type—had about the way the place should look. His *lokal* had the appearance of an ordinary Constantinople café, and its decoration and furniture, refined and modern at the same time, made an unforgettable impression.

Sometimes, as if from forgetfulness, the Hadji left a

small piece of hashish in his pocket or on one of the pieces of furniture, which gave one of the patrols the satisfaction of uncovering it. The punishment for such a small amount was insignificant and Old Minas confessed innocently that he had got it from the druggists for his personal use as a painkiller and sleeping-pill essential for someone of his old age. The patrolmen forgave him this, as among other things, he was known as "a man of God," as all present in the *teke* would willingly put their hands in the fire and swear. However, if on one of their raids they discovered any implements that indicated contraband hashish and its use at a *teke*, their achievement was much greater, and they were likely to receive generous *bakshish*. And their reports, depending on how much money had been given, would enable the owner to escape heavy punishment, or get off with a lighter one, though they still contained enough evidence to scare him.

The punishment could be terrible; beginning with the closing of the café, the confiscation and removal of all its contents and the imprisonment or exile of the owner. If among the patrol there was just one awkward officer who persisted in his suspicions, it was either from a sense of duty, or—and this was more likely—out of fanaticism, because the café was Greek-owned and he wanted its owner to be punished and humiliated. Thanks to his dignity and the respect he had acquired for his *teke*, Hadji Minas knew how to avoid such humiliation, while his "protectors," not wanting to be deprived of the enjoyments of the place, would intervene where necessary and make sure that the case was shelved, or better still, wiped from the record completely. This was done by a scribe simply running his tongue over what he had written with a reed pen dipped in the vegetable ink which was used for Turkish writing. So Hadji Minas would emerge pure from the licked clean paper of the Official Report. He was also helped by his friends when the *teke* was suddenly raided by the police. This would happen either early when the hash-smokers were gathering in the back-room for the mystic-rite, or at the end of the evening when they had enjoyed their "black" and their high had passed, giving way to the desire to eat and to drink good coffee while lounging in their seats. Above all, Minas wanted to avoid a raid taking place at the time the faithful were actually smoking. Such raids had the object of killing three birds with one shot: discovering the *teke* in full action, confiscating contraband hashish, and catching any wanted criminals among the smokers. But the Hadji, good-hearted by nature and compassionate to the underdog, didn't see any obligation to give up to the cops any of his addicts. He respected them all, of whatever social class or religion, and rightly considered them all faithful to the *teke*, which to him was a holy and inviolable place. In addition, life had taught him to regard any type of State, municipal or local authority officials as good-for-nothings who had no connection with honesty, humanity or justice.

Sometimes, because of bad communication between

Minas and his bribed policemen, or a sudden decision by the authorities to make an immediate raid, the Hadji was not warned in time to calmly take safety measures at the *teke*. As soon as his men who were keeping watch in the surrounding alleys noticed suspicious movements by the patrols or Local Police, they gave the danger signal by whistling a certain song, which was changed from time to time. The message passed from one to the other and reached the *teke* like lightning. There, all the helpers and hash-smokers, led by the Old Man, hurriedly hid anything that smacked of a *teke*. Hadji Minas hid the *nargiles* and every other implement connected with hash-smoking. To get rid of the smell of hashish, a couple of the helpers threw sugar, lemon leaves, incense and one or two whole apples onto the braziers. Others prepared coffee, tea, tobacco pipes and sherbets and laid them on the *sala* tables together with small plates of roasted almonds, hazelnuts and pistachios, along with dishes of almond-flavoured *lokum*, all of which they took ready-prepared from low cupboards placed under the divans.

The appearance of the *sala* was altered in a flash, like a scene change in a theatre. The customers had taken up their positions lounging on the divans and in the chairs and were enjoying what was laid before them while smoking their cigarettes or tobacco pipes. In the meantime, any wanted persons had disappeared through the doors of the rear yard. Everything was changed and pleasant, ready to greet the police like welcome customers: and when they made their entrance they discovered the Old Man and his assistants casually serving the customers of the "café" with whatever might be drunk or eaten at The City's other cafés or at the Sublime Porte, or even by the Padişah—the Sultan himself. Hadji Minas's café differed from others not only in the originality of its decoration, but in certain austere ways which impressed the Turks, simple citizens and Government Officials alike, and consolidated his reputation as a "*namuslu adam*," an "honourable man," which naturally was reflected on his business.

The Old Man had been initiated into the mysteries of hashish since childhood, knew all its properties, and as a master of his craft felt responsible for the condition of his customers. That's why he didn't allow the use of any form of alcohol in the *teke*, even when the smokers had passed through their high and come around perfectly. This was for the good of their health and to ensure they got full enjoyment from the hashish. He made this rule well-known to all and kept to it to show his respect for Mohamed who cursed alcohol as the work of Satan and forbade it to his followers; a religious ruling not upheld by many Turkish cafés, which secretly served rakı and cognac. Thus, the reports on "Searches for the Avoidance of State Revenue" verified that at the *kafene* of Hadji Minas "Order and the Rule of Law" prevailed. This was contributed to by the dignified behaviour of the hash-smokers, either instinctively or coached by Old Minas, and the way he honoured his visitors. In that pleasant environment with its beautiful pictures on the walls and its strange ceiling the Upholders of the Law were happy to sit for a while and rest from their arduous labours. But to amuse his daring nature, Minas encouraged them to carry out their duty and search his *lokal* thoroughly. He encouraged them to look wherever they wished and opened any hidden place they asked him to. In this way they obtained enough data to make out a full report. It was of great importance for the present and future of the business that the report stated that after the strictest searches of all corners of the premises nothing suspicious had been found. When the time came for them to depart, having found nothing, the Hadji would offer them either cigarettes made from the finest quality tobacco and contraband cigarette-paper, or sweets for their children, which they—in reality poor men with golden insignia of rank—accepted with great pleasure and with many good wishes to the Hadji-Baba. When it happened that an officer of high rank was amongst them, Minas made him a suitable gift—a one hundred pound bank-note, or a small keg of sealed "Koniak Phinopoulou" or "Barbaresou"; the famed "Yunan Konyak," the "Greek Cognac" which the Turks, and the Egyptians, preferred to the French variety, even the famous Martell. The French had started a diplomatic struggle to forbid the Greeks from using the attractive word "Koniak" on their labels, supposedly because that was the name of a town in France, Cognac, which had the unique right to use the word. In fact, the good quality of the Greek cognac had ruined the French profits.

. . .

When the small sanctum had filled and the faithful had settled into a circle close together, silent with their gleaming eyes fixed on the *nargiles*, the Hadji looked slowly around embracing each one in turn with his glance and said warmly, "Maşallah, maşallah, yavrumlar — Bless you, my children." After completing his inspection of the faithful, he offered a ready prepared *nargile* to whoever happened to be in front of him, taking a last draw himself to make sure everything was in order.

The *nargile* made its round of the smokers, passing from hand to hand. At first the draws contained more hashish and were short and shallow. The smoker had to take in with each draw just the amount of hashish that his organism desired. As they continued, the draws became deeper and louder as the hashish became less and the addict sought an increased amount. The Hadji—who understood the needs of the smokers—regulated the number of *nargiles* so that one followed the other rhythmically, there was not too long between one draw and the next and the smokers could enjoy the hashish and its effect on their bodies and minds.

Some smoked awkwardly, holding the bowl of the *nargile* with one hand and the pipe in the other; these were the novices. The experienced addicts held the bowl in both hands, like something beloved, and drew with all their soul, their heads bent forward over their chests. At every draw their cheeks blew out like empty goatskins and their appearance was distorted with eyes bulging and fixed on the *nargile*. Some remained with that expression even when not holding the pipe; silent with their palms open and an oafish look of complaint, as if something valuable had been taken from them. Others, when the *nargiles* had left them, let out stifled noises of pleasure, short like hiccups. Those who were squatting, sitting on the ground or kneeling had their heads and arms raised as if waiting for something to fall to them from heaven or were in awe of something unseen.

Sometimes the draws were accompanied by choked coughs, tears in the eyes or spitting on the packed earth floor. This was done by those who were inexperienced, and they then felt ashamed and feared the masters of the art would despise them; but in fact, the old hands gave encouragement and Minas showed them how to draw on the pipe.

The smoke which was emitted from the pipes and the mouths of the smokers gradually filled the small enclosed space. The complete silence which reigned in there was disturbed only by the bubbling of water in the *nargiles*, while the aroma of the hashish, the *karışık* and the *sade* grew stronger, and mixed with the breath of the aroused smokers, made the atmosphere heavy. When the hashish in the *nargile* was nearly finished, various smokers begged in hoarse voices: "Hacı, bir daha — Hadji, one more" and quick as a flash Minas replaced the exhausted *nargile* with another which he had prepared and tested. The change had to take place quickly as the others watched in suspense; you'd think the break, if it was extended, would spoil their enjoyment. Sometimes the Old Man asked one of the addicts to help him prepare the new pipe, as if he'd seen that hidden desire in his eyes. The others envied him the honour, hoping that if Allah wished it so their turn would come. From time to time during the smoking the Hadji would go into the *sala* and verify with signals to his guards that order, peace and safety prevailed all around.

After smoking for quite a while, the hash-smokers began to make quick, successive draws on the pipe in an uncontrolled way and didn't want to part with the *nargile.* This was the sign that they were getting high and being overcome by the *dalga*—the "wave" of the hashish. In this condition several of them withdrew and quietly made their own way to the *sala*. Others stopped smoking and left after exchanging glances with the Hadji or after a gently spoken word from him. When somebody felt a heavy *dalga* but wanted to continue smoking, the Old Man approached him, tapped him on the shoulder and led him to the *sala* saying: "That's enough, yavrum. That's enough. We'll be here again." The smoker, whoever he might be, obeyed respectfully.

As each one left, he silently saluted, placing his right palm on his chest and inclining his head slightly, first to the Hadji and then to the others. However, there were always some who were in such a state that they were unable to walk out without help; while others with heavy, trembling steps made their way silently into the *sala*. There in that phantasmagorical world—in contrast to the small, bare smoking area where they were crowded together—they could comfortably enjoy the ecstatic delights of their pipe dreams.

Under the *dalga* of the hashish which affected their brains, their bodies and their souls, each one took up the position which suited him on the divans and the simple low chairs. Some, as if their bodies were so heavy that they could not command them, only just managed to fall wherever it might be, like heaps of flabby flesh without skeletons to support them. In contrast, others held themselves lithely and took up proud poses; while others leaned against their neighbours like abandoned parcels. Several were curled up and appeared to be sleeping and a few were sitting with their bodies tensed, their legs stretched wide, their arms behind their heads and their clothes unbuttoned as if they needed space and air. Of those who were sitting in chairs, most had their arms and legs spread wide, resting on the seats beside them. Some faces were calm and happy, others expressionless or even uneasy and twitching. The eyes of some were bright and opened wide, others seemed to be covered with a misty cloudiness, while others looked around through half-closed lids, their pupils shining. A very few were withdrawn and sunken-cheeked as though ill. The eyes of others flickered here and there as if trying to find somewhere to rest. Several had their mouths half-open, like idiots, with the bottom lip hanging heavy and wet from the small amount of froth which dribbled from the corner. Most however, had their mouths tight shut to hold in the aromatic liquid of the hashish as it welled up from their guts and which they swallowed down again, spasmodically shaking their bodies, arms and legs not moving from the position they had first taken up. From time to time they made as if to move into a more comfortable position, but rarely managed it. All of these small and difficult movements were reflected in their faces by grimaces which gave some trace of life to those creatures enervated by smoking and overcome by psychoneurotic hallucinations.

Slowly, under the influence of the hashish which steadily increased, working on their bodies and on their psyches, the satiated, rested smokers began to come around, to awaken from their lethargy. Their first movement was to open their eyes wide and to look all around slowly and vaguely like half-wits. When their glance fell on the framed pictures, they gazed at them fixedly with a strange expression. From there their eyes moved upwards to the ceiling and passed across its multiform world, the meeting with which threw them into all sorts of psychical states. Many were engrossed in those exotic heavens, staring upwards in silent, open-mouthed wonder. Several looked at the hanging objects questioningly and suspiciously; others seemed overcome by amazement and let out stifled exclamations of wonder and awe. Quite a few let their eyes roam over every inch of the ceiling searching for the object of their desire, and when it was found crossed their arms and let out a deep, relieved, "Och." A few, as if terrified by the sight of so many different things, turned their heads away, but still gave sideways, secret glances as if watching out for something. But most of them, before that vision of a fantastic yet real suspended world, fell at once into ecstasy, adjusting their bodies to enjoy it more comfortably, peering with wonder and fixing their eyes on the point which attracted them the most, their minds slowly working, their souls at peace.

With eyes resting on whatever gave them delight, they removed their amber worry-beads from their pockets and began to pass the beads through their fingers with a slow, rhythmic clicking which accompanied their musings and echoed lightly in the silence of the *sala*, while smiles sweetened their tired faces. The poorer ones turned small pieces of chain between their fingers. Each of them was transported by his ecstatic illusions and envisaged who knows what desires, what dreams, what longings lodged in the depths of his being.

When all the smokers had gathered in the *sala* and each was lounging in his place, Hadji Minas would enter. He gave them all an encouraging look, saying cheerfully and in a praising voice, as if awarding prizes: "Maşallah! Maşallah! Aferim. Aferim. Kardaşlar, yavrumlar," that is to say, "Glory be to God! Bravo, bravo! My brothers, my children." Then he would light the double wick of the central lamp and raise it till the flame lit the pictures on the walls more clearly. With the help of his young assistants he also lit the many-coloured lanterns that were scattered across the hanging world of the ceiling and illuminated it with their sparkling brilliance. Finally, he opened the transom-windows over the windows which gave onto the front yard and also those of the two doors of the *sala*, one of which gave onto the front yard while the other led to the "rear shop" and from there through another wide-open door into the rear yard.

In the breeze that was created by the opening of the doors and windows, all the hanging objects began to stir like a crowd suddenly coming to life, pulsing with many colours, some bright as lightning, others shimmering like stars. All, either singly or knocking against each other two by two or more, made various sounds, sometimes quietly like a children's choir, sometimes loudly like a brass band letting out loud bass or treble notes. The paper objects seemed to be whispering secretly to each other and the ivory things spoke discretely, interrupted by sudden silences. The metal objects clanged, you'd think the glass ones were singing free from care, while the wooden things kept time with deep thuds. From time to time sounds like high-pitched cries came from the ringing bells. This woke the caged birds from their lethargy, and they added their voices to the polyphony, at first quietly and then, like tenors or prima donnas, increasing their volume until they dominated the sounds of that strange orchestra. Amidst this airborne exotic world of many colours and sounds sailed the five ships; their sails open and filled by the breeze they swayed from side to side as if plying a celestial sea between heaven and earth.

When the draught was not strong enough to set the

hanging objects in motion, Hadji Minas would skilfully pass his hand, lightly or more heavily over some of them to strengthen the impression they made on the enraptured smokers. Again, when there was no wind at all and nothing moved, the Hadji would take the hand-bellows—made of the large, strong wings of a turkey-cock bound in the shape of a half-open fan to a short handle—and pass them closely over all those paper, glass, wooden, metal or bone objects, sometimes blowing strongly, sometimes lightly, filling the *sala* like an experienced maestro with sounds and harmonies of his own inspiration. These pleasing sounds and music made the deepest impression on the trippers with beneficial effects on their psychical condition, their dreams and fantasies. With this prototypical concert the *sala* took on a new atmosphere. All those who were in a state of lethargic ecstasy began to move as though the sounds caused waves of arousal to move within them, making veins pulse, electrifying the nerves and stimulating the body to bring the limbs back to life. It was as if they were being reborn into a new existence. Then were heard deep sighs, joyful exclamations, murmured conversations ending in quiet laughter, low-voiced recitations, sobs, quiet weeping and stifled cries. In that *sala*, that warm and intimate environment with its enchanting pictures, under that hazy sky with its imaginary world which pulsed with light as if alive and gave off sounds and movement as though dancing, all those men, old, middle-aged, young were overcome by a psychoneurotic sensitivity, a bodily tranquillity; if only fleetingly, they meditated, dreamed, were delighted or impassioned, living in happy companionship.

Their faces relaxed with joyful delight; their eyes shone with an internal light. When some picked out in that heavenly world their own particular dream-fantasy they greeted it with hand or eye while their mouths formed silent words. Others spoke directly to the visions that confronted them as if expecting to be told a tender secret. A few remained silent, their bodies relaxed, with their eyes fixed on whatever electrified their imaginations and moved their souls. One, bewitched by the visions he saw up there, shook violently every now and again and stretched his arms upward to reach it without success; eventually he rose quietly from his seat, hunched over to become small and invisible and went quickly and silently to touch the object which drew him so urgently, then ran back lightly and happily to his seat. Two or three stared blankly at the heavenly ceiling or one of the pictures, their bodies still as though mesmerised by what they saw, the slow and delicate movements of their fingers revealing their inner joy. Another, upright, his head held high, watched the progress of his vision until an ungovernable force drew him from his seat and with arms extended like a sleepwalker, he moved to take hold of it. Among them all there was one who wished to do other than sit gazing at the ceiling; he marked time spasmodically with small rhythmic steps, his body pulsing as if made of rubber.

These were the blessed hashish smokers who enjoyed the magical unction of "good hashish," the privileged who saw in that Gök-dünya—that Celestial World, wonderful visions calling them to join them up there and others gesturing that they would come down to them. They were the fortunate smokers who felt themselves light as their dream-fantasies and identified with those exciting illusions which stimulated their brains, brought relief to their souls and a calm invigoration to their bodies. Their facial expressions, their glances, their gestures and their few words all revealed that—all together in pleasant company—they were travelling through the indefinable world of the ceiling and the more realistic one of the pictures.

But there were addicts who had been struck by "bad hashish." At first their expressions were sad, then uneasy and then, as though they were suddenly confronted by something terrifying, they became aggressive. Sometimes one of them let out a piercing scream, and with his arms made as if to defend himself from some invisible enemy he could see flying secretly among the world of the ceiling. From the time the hash-smokers assembled in the *sala*, Hadji Minas was on the move here and there, watching their condition closely as they surfaced from the narcotic depths. He watched with especial care those who showed worrying signs of any bad influence of the hashish, ready to forestall any unpleasant outburst that might disturb the euphoria enjoyed by the other smokers there in the warm atmosphere of the *teke*; as the place was the pride and joy of his old age.

On one occasion, a smoker of bad hashish who had risen from his seat and run around after the vision that was tormenting him, let out a piercing cry, covered his face with his arms and crashed unconscious to the ground. Who knows in what horrifying way his vision had ended. The Old Hadji, the master of all situations, lifted him to his feet with sure hands and gave him a hard smack on both cheeks; which immediately became as red as Dutch cheese, having been as pale as death. He then swabbed his face with plenty of rakı, which brought him round. The sufferer was embarrassed, kissed the Hadji's hand with tears in his eyes and begged his forgiveness. The Old Man jokingly restored his courage and made him laugh, finally kissing him on the forehead and saying, "You'll soon get over it. It's nothing my child."

Among the smokers there were sometimes one or two who wanted to smoke a *nargile*, a pipe or a cigarette before the time permitted by Hadji Minas and would not be denied. In such cases, he would allow only the cigarette, as it was the least strong, and would insist on sharing it with them and one or two others, "my puff, your puff," to keep to the minimum the effect of the tobacco on their organisms and to prevent its interfering with the normal effect of the hashish, especially during the time when the smokers were returning to normal. However, alcoholic drinks, even the lightest, were forbidden to everyone within Hadji Minas's Teke, whoever he might be; a rule which everyone knew and respected because they knew from experience the unbending will of the Old Man would not be changed, and that it was done for the good of their health and so they would fully enjoy the *mavraki*—the hashish.

When Hadji Minas judged that the faithful were becoming satiated and their enjoyment was lessening, he decided it was time for something new and different. Then, with the help of one or two of his assistants, he closed the upper shutters and told the others to bring in the animals from the yard: Asimi the silver goat, Yabandji the dog, the two cats Psipsina and Niarniari, his "Hero" the cockerel with his *sultanes*, and the rest. He let them loose in the *sala* where they wandered freely, following their habits and instincts. The doves flew here and there alighting sometimes on an object hanging from the ceiling, sometimes on the shoulder of a hash-smoker. The chickens spread out right and left searching tirelessly for something to peck, while the cock, the "Kahraman," proudly approached his *sultanes* one by one, crowing menacingly like a satrap as though he were trying to forestall any unfaithfulness on the part of his harem. The cats, their tails upright and their eyes half-closed, meowed quietly and rubbed against the legs of the hash-smokers seeking their caresses and their warmth. The dog, Yabandji, went sniffing from one to another. He stood before each smoker, raised his head, looked him in the eye, and with a friendly bark sought a pat. The presence of the animals, the noise and movement, communicated its liveliness and joyful intimacy to the smokers. In the meantime, Minas had prepared something for each animal to eat, and the smokers, their minds now clearer but still under the light influence of the hashish, occupied themselves with that. They called the animals to them, gave them food from their hands, petted them, played with them, spoke to them and kissed them with tender joy. Some wanted to keep those good creatures forever near them, but the animals, as they had been taught, left each one and went to another as if they wished to try the love and caresses of all. True Easterner that he was, Old Hadji Minas never allowed his wife or daughter to enter the *teke* and none could say that they had even once set eyes on them.

As the minutes passed in that closed space full of men, the re-breathed smells of hashish and tobacco, the flowers, plants and fruit giving off their sweet aromas combined with the breath and odours of the animals, caused the atmosphere to become thick and heavy. The animals were the first to suffer a reaction, as if they were high too. Their eyes became cloudy, their heads heavy and they moved and walked stumblingly. The birds sang weakly and irregularly as if tired, as if they had lost the melody or even their voices. The lamps became dimmer from the mists of heat and the half-light from the ceiling descended lower and lower creating a new atmosphere in the *sala*. As the smokers came round they felt a pleasant psychical satiety, a simple organic relaxation, an almost sensual bodily languor which cast them into a tranquil Nirvana.

Hadji Minas, who considered these moments among the most beautiful, left them in this happy state for as long as it took to return the animals to their dens and to place in the braziers and lighters balsamic resins which smelled sweetly, cleared the atmosphere, awakened the senses and invigorated tired nerves. Then the Old Hadji and his helpers brought in with full pomp and circumstance all the fresh and sparkling-clean delicacies his "High Class Lokal" could provide: tasty Yemen coffee, fragrant Persian tea, sherbets and syrups from the East, cigarettes, pipes with sweet tobacco from Xanthi, *nargiles* with sweet-smelling fine-cut Isfahan tobacco, fresh almonds and pistachios from Chios, *lokum* from Syros, sweets from the finest confectioners in The City, rose-water and potions prepared by his wife and daughter. All in abundance and what the heart of every smoker desired. As the Old Man placed them on the tables he praised each drink or food with a few quietly sung words which the smokers replied to with, "Mm, mm, och, aman," as though already devouring the delicacies with their eyes. When all had been richly served he stood in the middle of the *sala* and clapped his hands—loudly, softly, loudly, softly—in a rhythm now quick, now slow as if calling them to the dance, and chanted happily: "Hop-hop, yavrumlar, buyurun arkadaşlar, yeyin, için, kardaşlar," which means, "Come forward my children, at your service comrades, eat, drink my brothers."

Then the smokers began to joyfully eat and drink the riches spread out before them, slowly so as to appreciate everything fully. In the meantime, the Old Man went around the *sala* with a few pleasant words or a joke for each one in his good-hearted way. If it was a strongly built fellow, he would slap him on the back exclaiming with wonder, "May you live long, my lion!" To another who might still appear in a dreamy state, he would look into his eyes and exclaim laughing, "Aşık delikanlı seni! – Hey, you, amorous young man!"

And if it was someone with problems he would caress his head, saying tenderly, "We are here, my child," to give him courage.

All the smokers had such faith in Hadji Minas that at every stage of the rites they awaited his words and commands as though he were a wizard who knew how to satisfy their every psychical desire. In his own way he got them to enjoy the hashish fully, as much when they were smoking it as in the later moments of their high, which passed pleasantly with various entertaining invocations, until much later when it was time for them to leave. In all of the food and drink, as with the tobacco, the Hadji placed a very small amount of hashish as an antidote. A measure which helped those organisms, tired by neuro-psychical stimulation to recover their balance in a calm way and readjust to life with a smooth rhythm. Eating and drinking in that pleasant atmosphere and in a joyful mood, the pallor left their faces and was replaced by the freshness of recovery. The strength returned to their movements and mood. However, a few remained apathetic as if day-dreaming nostalgically of what they had enjoyed, but which now already belonged to the past. Those are moments when the psyche and the mind of a hash-smoker float in an emptiness and must be filled anew, giving an end to what they had lived and a beginning to what they would experience returning to everyday life.

It was exactly then that there appeared before the astounded eyes of the smoker a living drama, a concentration, an apotheosis of the uncanny experience they had lived in that fairytale retreat. At a moment when the smokers were completely relaxed the Hadji would disappear, to return minutes later accompanied by the majestic and proud peacock. Once back in the *sala*, the Old Man—a skilful manipulator of the souls of men and animals—persuaded the creature with words and caresses, and a special fodder, to open its long, polymorphous wings into a huge, triumphant, golden-coloured halo which transformed it all at once into a magnificent idol. Its dazzle filled the *sala* and the smokers were overcome with ecstasy and wonder. The peacock, like an actor sure of his glamour and beauty and the power of his art, proudly followed Minas's movements. He went forward a little, stood still, turned slowly right and left, beautiful and haughty, with small steps. It seemed he was preparing to radiate his brilliant colouring, the bewitching luminosity of his incomparable costume. Then suddenly he let out a harsh, shrill noise like a cry of despairing triumph, after which the Hadji removed that divine vision which the smokers had enjoyed as a final reflection of all the pleasurable feelings and sights they had experienced in the *teke*.

• • •

After that final vision, the Old Hadji led the smokers back to everyday life. Speaking of the peacock, he reminded them of the wondrous works of Allah which mankind was able to enjoy and mentioned as examples old tales of mythical heroes that were loved by the faithful and stimulated their imagination. He mentioned past and present events that aroused their curiosity. He did this walking around slowly and standing before one or another of them and addressing him so as to draw him into the talk. He recited verses and short extracts from the Koran or sayings and proverbs loved by the people of the East. He told them short and cheerful anecdotes and asked them risqué questions to draw out humorous answers and provoke laughter. With these wiles he encouraged indiscreet talk and so, without jarring changes, the smokers were drawn calmly and jokingly back into normal life in a warm and intimately friendly environment. They ordered more drinks and food, which the young helpers brought, and began talking in small groups. At first various subjects were discussed, but slowly the great interest in one story and the lively way it was being told would draw them into a larger group. The Hadji encouraged the eloquent tale-teller: "Naklet. Naklet Kardaşım. Aman! – Tell on. Tell on my brother!"

The narrator usually began with some description of the amazing journeys and feats of "Sevach Thalassinos" or Sinbad the Sailor, hilarious anecdotes about Nasredin Hodja, the amazing or ridiculous exploits of Karagöz, or similar tales of the Arabs, Greeks, Armenians and other peoples of the East. But the tales that drew the greatest interest were those of the incredible adventures and feats of legendary heroes; magnificent, but not lacking humorous episodes, or the exploits of simple and comic characters which caused the listeners to laugh heartily. Sometimes the whole story was improvised by the narrator, or was a repetition of what he had heard from another teller of tales. If this new material pleased the listeners, it became part of popular lore, thus enriching the old tradition with the new popular spirit of the age.

When the tale was finished, the comments and discussion which followed prepared the ground for the next one. Thus the joy of the word united all those different people. Often the narrator was transformed into an actor, he rose from his seat, advanced into the centre of the *sala* and there in a ringing voice, his eyes and expression altered, moving his hands and body, he became another person, inspired, moved by the fantastic adventures of the heroes of his story. Alone, he played out all the roles and with pantomime movements described the scenes where the wonderful events took place. Then, all the smokers would gather round, tightly bunched together, to get a better view of this extempore actor. They listened motionless in devout silence, their faces expressing the various emotions created by the exciting tales brought to life before them so skilfully by the narrator.

It was a strange thing. There in that *teke*, amongst so many men, in the psychical condition they were in, seeking moments of ecstatic exaltation, there was no place for erotic stories. If in the tales being told there happened to befall an erotic episode, it was intended to emphasise the chivalrous nature of the hero. In all these narrations there were no swear words, no blasphemy, no indecent innuendos or filthy carryings on. One could say that under the influence of hashish the smokers had been purified. A modest manliness prevailed in all of their words and behaviour which would not tolerate any coarseness. In all those men from different social classes and with radically different perceptions there bloomed an inherent dignity. Under Hadji Minas's roof, thanks to the way he treated everyone with a strict but friendly humanity, and thanks to the atmosphere of intimate geniality which he created for their enjoyment, all rediscovered those inborn virtues which life—for some wretched, for others corrupted—had buried in the depths of their being.

The stories also gave rise to poems and songs. Then the Hadji suddenly remembered the magic of music—which he loved as much as hashish—and took down the bouzouki and the tambourine and entrusted them to hands which knew how to bring forth from those singing instruments every kind of melody, some full of nostalgic longing, others sparkling and lively, but above all suited to accompany the sweet-voiced singer chosen by the Old Man. The voice and art of the *hanende*—the master-singer, brought to life passionate *gazeller*, nostalgic *manedes*, and melodic songs which gifted the smokers with a supreme delight that shook and at the same time calmed their souls and bodies. The singer's voice rose rich and pure, as did those of the smokers when the song demanded the accompaniment of a small chorus. There was none of the wild shouting that took place in other establishments. All respected the tranquility that reigned in that unique and almost holy refuge created by Hadji Minas. When the song had ended, the instruments began to play a dance melody in heavy and manly rhythm, a *zeïbekiko*, and not a *tsifteteli* or a *karsilamas*. The dancer, whoever he might be, removed his jacket and shoes and danced alone, free to improvise as his inspiration led him, remaining faithful however to the meaning of the music and its rhythm. As his friends became enthused they accompanied him, clapping lightly and rhythmically, occasionally uttering an encouraging, "Yaşa babayiğit — Yeia sou levendi!"

In the meantime the hours had rolled by. It was well past midnight. Dawn was approaching. The time had come for the pleasant company to break up. Hadji Minas saw written on the faces of the smokers tired expressions indicating the longing for sleep. Then, in his deep voice, he gave the signal for departure: "Kardaşlar, yavrumlar — Brothers, children, the time is right," adding some little joke and a promise about the next ritual.

One by one, amid the general stirring, the faithful made the decision to leave. They arranged their ruffled clothes, exchanged a few words, said farewell to each other, their right hands on their chests, heads slightly lowered, uttered an "Allahaısmarladık — Goodbye" and left in small groups with heavy steps. Some of the poorer ones chatted for a while to delay their departure from under that warm roof, which was perhaps the only pleasant refuge in their joyless lives; since only there could they freely live their dreams and enjoy themselves, if only for a short while. Hadji Minas was then obliged to clap his hands together loudly and raise his voice to the lingerers, "That's all my friends. Time to go!"

On the way out, each one threw his share onto a tray which the Old Man had placed by the outer door of the *sala*. Old Minas had worked out the total cost—hashish, drinks, food—and divided it into equal parts for all. The poorer had a whip-round to pay, but when the Hadji sometimes saw that they didn't have enough he did them a favour. The well-off always threw in extra and often some rich person, to give thanks for what he had enjoyed in there with his hash-smoking friends, and especially to show his respect for Hadji Minas, threw in a golden Turkish pound, saying modestly "All for you Hadji Baba."

Then others thanked him and the penniless loudly wished him: "May God give it to you in abundance!"

The ritual of hashish had come to its end quietly in the dawn hours. Usually, at the time when Old Minas and his young assistants had shut the *teke* and put away the most essential items, there would sail up to the door one of the most famous hash-smokers in that Boundless City, that Paradise of the Passionate. An Arab, mature, tall and upright as a date tree in the desert, as spirited and alert as an Arabian thoroughbred. Always cleanly dressed in a close-fitting silk and wool jellaba, dark-blue with yellow stripes and tightly bound at the waist with a wide violet-coloured cummerbund. His face, with the strong features of his race, glowed under his orange turban. He sold *aşure* —wheat juice with sugar, dried fruit and nuts—in small, coloured containers lined up on a rough wooden table and covered with a spotlessly clean white kerchief. He carried this in a breezy manner on his head, supporting it when the time came on a wooden tripod which he carried over his right shoulder while his left arm swung rhythmically with his stride. He announced his passing and his goods by crying loudly: "Lop! Lop! Lop!" according to him, "Fresh! Fresh as can be!"

People, Turks and Greeks, shouted after him "Arap! Arap!" as they shouted at the black dogs in the street. He didn't get angry, but laughed and joked continually and had a good word for everybody. As soon as he arrived at the *teke*, Hadji Minas opened the door to him and received him like a close friend. They greeted each other warmly, their palms entwined, as they respected each other greatly. The Hadji went immediately to the rear room and prepared the pipes. The Arab followed him, tapping various of the hanging objects as he passed and laughing at the sounds produced, while the young assistants saluted him respectfully and greeted him—"At your service Selim Aga"—like an important person. If, as sometimes happened, he arrived before the last hashish smokers had left, they greeted him with special warmth and respect. All the addicts admired him because he had the fame—and it was the truth—of being able to smoke pure hashish night and day without showing the slightest sign of torpor. Just the opposite, he was always lively and warm-hearted. The two experienced smokers took their first pipe standing opposite each other, silent and unmoving, looking one another directly in the eye mirthfully. When the first pipe was finished, the Arab smoked another on his own while they chatted. The Hadji didn't charge him, and the "Uzun Arab"—the Tall Arab, as he was also known, gave him in exchange several packets of *aşure*. Enough for Minas and his wife and daughter, with some left over for the peacock and a few of the other animals.

As soon as he had finished his second pipe, "The Wonderful Selim," as Minas called him with admiration, announced his departure in a voice as loud as a steamship's whistle. He placed the table on his head, picked up the tripod and left fresh and cheerful with his body swaying like a sheet of metal plating; and without caring that it was very late, long past midnight with dawn approaching, set off through the alleyways crying out in his ringing voice, "Lop! Lop! Lop!" awakening the people of Constantinople from their sweet pre-dawn sleep.

ELEVEN

Yahudi Doktor Effendi

During those years the downhill road Sakız-Ağaç, one of the most central in Stavrodromi, or Beyoğlu, was inhabited by Christians, Greeks in the majority, and the lower part was not yet paved. It hadn't even been banked up with earth, and when it rained it turned into a stream as all the water from the surrounding narrow streets descended there. When the periodical heavy rains really set in—they lasted for days—it became a torrent, over-flowing and flooding shops and homes. The force of the water uprooted trees and carried away furniture, clothes and all sorts of things, frequently animals, sometimes even people. From there the waters emptied into a large *dere*—the gully of Yeni Şehir—at the bottom of the hills. This *dere* bounded on the West the hills of Stavrodromi and was where all the alleys and lanes ended which branched off from that side of the Great Street of Pera; La Grande Rue de Pera as it was known to the Europeans.

The gully of Yeni Şehir emptied into the Golden Horn at the small plain of Kasim Pasha and that was where the worst happened. A wide area all around was flooded and turned into a muddy green swamp where myriads of insects hummed, with unpleasant consequences for the surrounding area, which was heavily populated by the poor of every race. The Local Government decided to carry out "Sewage Works" and empty the swamp water into the Golden Horn; they did this with such zeal that before it dried out completely the next heavy rains came and the swamp filled up again, to the great joy of the local children who splashed about in there, and of the insects which sucked their blood.

Down there, at the bottom of Sakız-Ağaç near the edge of the gully, a Jewish "practical doctor" had his pharmacy and consulting-room, a single room over an unused shop, which was half-underground and was flooded every time the rains came. An outside staircase of some ten steps led up to a roofed veranda and the pharmacy's entrance.

This follower of Hippocrates was an elderly Israelite, very clever, bony, with long hands and thin fingers, a hooked nose and short beard. He was a careful, serious and good-hearted person, who always wore a low, dark fez and a black coat, which he removed in the consulting-room and replaced with a spotless white robe. When examining a patient, he slipped his gold-rimmed glasses to the end of his nose to peer closely with his sky-blue eyes, which shone like a clear sky and mirrored his kindness and patience.

His glance was calm but penetrating and inspired courage and belief. Nobody knew his name. People of every race and religion came to him and despite the enmity and prejudices which many people up to a point had against the Jews, everyone respected "Yahudi Doktor Effendi," as they called him.

Among his many patients were the sick of all social classes: modest householders, craftsmen, workers, all sorts of poor people, even the rich, Muslims, Christians both Orthodox and unorthodox, an assortment of the human race. He treated them all in the same way, without any discrimination. He was so capable and had obtained such fame that even though without a diploma he was officially allowed to practise "The Art of Healing," as he modestly called it. People said he had performed miracles; had cured those whom Licensed Practitioners had given up as doomed to die. Many of the latter, moved by jealousy and fear for their businesses, employed every means to hinder him from "making a laughingstock of their exalted science," as they vainly said. The faith of the ordinary people who had received nothing but good from him and the esteem of the rich whom he had cured counteracted these machinations. Again, because he didn't give prescriptions and made up the medicines himself, another group of well-wishers, the "Certified Pharmacists", with the aid of the doctors, demanded that strict analyses should be made of his medicines by the State Laboratory. All were found to be correctly made from natural substances, without chemicals.

The only room, which was quite large, was where he both examined his patients and made up the medicines. On the rear wall, in a glass-fronted cabinet, were rows of gleaming white porcelain jars on shelves. They contained his medicines: herbs he ordered from villagers, roots and barks that he bought in the Mısır Çarşı, the Egyptian Bazaar, and minerals from the wholesale drugstores. On each jar, in red, blue or black ink, he wrote in large letters the name of each medication in Turkish or Hebrew, Latin or Greek, sometimes with capital letters. On other jars he had made clumsy sketches of leaves, flowers, animals, insects, fish and reptiles. All represented medicines whose therapeutic capabilities were known only to Doktor Effendi.

Not far in front of the cabinet was a long, narrow table like a bench where he prepared the medicines. In the middle of its white marble top, under glass, stood small bronze scales like a toy on which he weighed his medicines. On one side of them were laid out two or three small-to-medium sized marble mortars, and on the other rounded bottles of coloured medical syrups. At one end of the bench, supported on a wooden frame, was a small glass barrel of distilled water and at the other a copper basin where he washed his instruments and hands. Everything was spotless. Long benches, like those in an old-fashioned school, ran along the walls with only a small gap for people to enter and exit. The benches were always full of all sorts: old men and women, mothers with children and babies, young men and girls. All the Tribes of Israel were there: Turks, Greeks, Levantines, Armenians, Jews, even Gypsies and Arabs. Every race with their characteristic mugs, their dress, their ways, their local dialects. A crowd which came from every corner of the Boundless City, from as far as the name had spread of Yahudi Doktor, who gave strength to the sick and the hope of a cure.

They came at the break of dawn, even before the doctor who was always early. When it happened that he was late, because of going to buy medicines or because he was on visits—he was even called to the mansions of Pashas—crowds gathered waiting outside the pharmacy, on the stairs, on the veranda, as if on pilgrimage. Something similar must have happened round the Baptismal Font of Solomon in Jerusalem and the Asklipeion of Epidaurus in olden times and still happens today at Tinos and at Lourdes in France.

He would examine each patient in turn, there where they sat beside each other after he had made space for them to move freely. The only exceptions he made were for the seriously ill, whom he examined at once. He took their pulse, placed his hand behind the ear at the base of the neck to get their temperature, held their eyelids open and examined the eyes with great care and did the same to the mouth. He then listened to chest, back and sides through a long stethoscope, pressed with his fingers various parts of the body, asked about their trouble, their parents, their work and their lives, giving great importance as to whether they defecated regularly. He used no medical instruments, removed no growths, took no blood, changed no wound-dressings. When such things became necessary, he sent the patient to the barber Ventourelis; a friend of his from Mytilini who had his shop nearby and was famous for his light touch.

After examining each patient, he went behind the bench, washed and dried his hands carefully and immediately prepared their medication. He did the same when he returned from a visit to the house of a wealthy person, giving the medicine to one of their servants who had accompanied him. He took no money for examining his poor patients, only for the medicine. In those cases, he told them how much it cost and accepted whatever they gave him. However, those who could afford it paid what he considered enough and the rich rewarded him liberally. When during the course of his examination he observed the poverty of a patient he took no money at all. If the poor person was accompanied by a child, Yahudi Doktor Effendi always had something to offer, sweets or toys—and to all the sick children he told jokes and was tender and kind. The treatments he laid down were easy to follow and the medicines he prescribed were usually available to the poor, and when one was difficult to find he gave it from his own stock.

For those with chest complaints he ordered tight, hot compresses made from small bags of roasted bran on chest and back and the drinking of hot linden tea. For pains in the kidneys: the wearing of a cummerbund of unwashed wool against the flesh and the drinking of a hot infusion of rosemary all day in place of water. He brought down temperatures accompanied by bad headaches with very hot, salty foot baths, compresses of boiled linseed on the forehead, the wrists and the ankles, plus hot tea with cognac to make the patient sweat out the poisons. He fought coughs with hot drinks of *deniz–kataif*, that is to say seaweed. For sore eyes: washing with plenty of lukewarm water. For a sore throat: gargles with either hot salt-water or pure lemon juice followed by opening the mouth as wide as possible with the back of the middle finger. He relieved piles, before he shrunk them, by bathing the arse in piping hot bran-water, then applied plasters made from onions that he boiled on embers until they became an ointment. Something similar worked for eczema, which he bound lightly with fine burnt sugar spread on a sterilised kerchief. And more and more practical remedies...How could anyone remember them all? For every illness he had his remedies: powders, pills, drops, syrups, ointments, plasters, suppositories; and almost always a separate one to help the patient to defecate and to urinate abundantly. All were natural, from herbs, roots, barks, minerals; those for internal use smelled sweetly of dill-water or rose-water so as to be easily taken, especially by the children.

He spoke a language of his own, made up of Turkish, Ladino, Greek, and Levantinika, with weird syntax and a Jewish accent. He lived in Hasköy, a Jewish suburb–ghetto up the Golden Horn, and it took him an hour on foot to reach the Christian quarter, where he arrived early in the morning and worked all day, standing upright, until he could no longer see in the evening; he never lit a lamp. Regularly, every day except Saturday he came, in the cold, in heat waves, in rain and in snow to cure people of every religion and race in the Boundless City of many peoples.

One day Yahudi Doktor Effendi didn't come. The faithful waited for him patiently until nightfall, but he didn't appear. The thought that he might have come to some harm made them forget their own pains. They left uneasy. The next day the pharmacy again remained closed. In vain, they anxiously looked down the alleys to see if he was approaching. The same on the third day. All that growing crowd of poor people was eaten up with black fear. They were overcome with anxiety and several set out for Hasköy to try to get news of him, although none knew exactly where he lived. But their Yahudi Doktor Effendi would never come again; he had died. A beautiful death worthy of his good soul. That night he had gone to sleep, never to waken again. The great majority of the sick couldn't take it in, as they believed he who had saved so many from death would never die.

. . .

All those poor people: Greeks, Turks, Armenians, Jews, Gypsies, Arabs, an enormous crowd gathered there outside his pharmacy, all cried for Yahudi Doktor Effendi as if they had lost one of their own, their protector, their saviour and, with wringing hearts and tears, wished him from the depths of their souls: "Allah rahmet eylesin — May God grant him peace."

TWELVE

Sofu-Hadji-Thomas

He was my uncle, my father's eldest brother. His mother's family came from Fanar, the seat of the Orthodox Patriarchate, and he was proud of that. When the Turks, enraged by the outbreak of the Greek Revolution, hanged the Patriarch Gregory V the family moved to Feriköy, then one of the most distant small suburbs of The City.

His surname had been forgotten, because although people knew he was my father's brother they didn't use the family name, they just called him Sofu-Hadji-Thomas. He was quietly pleased about this as he had nothing in common with my father and didn't want to have anything to do with him, even with his "genealogical nomenclature" as he put it in the *katharevousa* or "high-Greek" which he used to mix into his conversation. Of that triple name, given to him by both Turks and Greeks, Sofu means in Turkish a pious, learned man and a Hadji is someone who has travelled to the Holy Lands: Mecca for the Muslims and Jerusalem for the Orthodox.

From his youth he had followed the tailor's craft. He worked capably and zealously, obtained a good name and by the time he was quite elderly had made a fair amount of money. He then gave up tailoring because, as he said, "He had got fed up with touching, even if only fleetingly, the hidden parts of the male body." He hadn't had the inspiration at a young enough age to become a Lady's Tailor and thus have the privilege of patting their bodies during fittings.

A few years after his demobilisation from tailoring he opened what he called "The Conversation Club," a strange sort of small café without a signboard in a quiet lane in the centre of the village. He did this not because he needed to work to make a living, but because he was a bachelor, alone and withdrawn from the world like a misanthrope and who felt the need to talk with various people when in the mood. So he organised the club in such a way that only people who could put up with the "eccentric Thomas"—as various snappish people called him and his strange ways—would find it interesting and want to visit regularly.

Before he opened the club, he had visited Jerusalem and become a Hadji. He no longer wore a hat, only a low black, brimless cap along with a dark black frock coat, buttoned up to the throat without a tie; like a "pseudo monk," as he called himself mockingly. But he disliked monks and priests so much that he avoided them in the street and didn't go to church so as not to hear or see them. However, as he saw it, he was religious and honoured the festivals, beliefs and rules of the Orthodox religion in his own ritual manner. He did this along with a slightly younger friend of his who had once been a priest and had become a layman, an action greatly respected by Hadji-Thomas. A "repentant priest" as they were called in The City, who lived from some small, undeclared and secret income. This friend copied Hadji-Thomas's way of dressing without having the title of "Hadji." Every Sunday and festival day the two of them, all alone, chanted—sometimes singly, sometimes together like cantors—the "holy words of the Christian day," standing upright before the iconostasis which my uncle had erected in his private room where he slept at the rear of the club.

The only icons he had were those of the Holy Trinity and the Holy Virgin; the latter was suckling the baby Christ with a bitter-sweet look, while his little hands were placed on her milk-swollen bare breasts. Two very old and tender icons created by the hand of a Byzantine painter. In front of them, day and night, a silver candlestick, as finely worked as lace, and a clay censer so that every afternoon the place was filled by the sweet smell of incense. On a shelf under the iconostasis a bundle slowly blackened. In it were the white shrouds and the black tomb candles my uncle had brought back from Jerusalem for the two of them. Because even though the "repentant priest" had not wanted to accompany my uncle on his pilgrimage to Jerusalem, Sofu-Thomas had brought back the grave clothes and candles for him as he wanted to enjoy his company in Paradise.

That was the uncle I knew and loved, the "Club President" as they called him, some seriously, others ironically. He was of average height, a little chubby but still firm-fleshed, not very talkative and calm in his movements. His face, with its regular features, always appeared thoughtful, somewhat serious and austere; frequently though, it would light up with tenderness, kindness and joy. His abundant white hair, aristocratic simplicity and neatness made him well-liked and respected.

His club was famed for its great variety of old wines and spirits. He offered nothing else to his customers. Not coffee and *lokum*, nor the rakı and meze so beloved by the Easterners. Only water, and you'd have to beg him for that. The drinks, their quality and the way you obtained them were strictly determined by the strange old "President." Each person drank what he wanted, sometimes served by Hadji-Thomas, sometimes by another habitué, sometimes by the drinker himself. Another of his quirks was to change the type of drink according to the topic being discussed, or to adjust the speed of consumption according to the direction the conversation was taking, or even to stop the drinking suddenly at a certain hour; tactics which tried the patience of his members and created a sort of tolerable status quo between him and them.

His basement was filled with bottles of old wine, spirits

and liqueurs sealed with cherry-coloured wax and stamped with the seal of the ring he wore on the first finger of his left hand. Its square stone, a green-black agate, hard as a diamond, was engraved with a Byzantine cross and four capital letters, S. H. T. Z., which stood for the initial letters of his triple name, Sofu-Hadji-Thomas, and his surname: Zarfis; the only case in which he would accept the use of this paternal name, and even then only the initial Z. The stone was by tradition considered *aimostatis*, which meant that if you revolved it firmly against a bleeding wound the blood would stop flowing. But the elderly Thomas, like his saintly namesake, didn't believe in such miracles and used the stone on his ring only to seal his wines and liqueurs. To each bottle he attached a white circular label, which he called the "navel," and on this he wrote in his own hand the name and chronology of the wine: Pasalimani, Koumandaria, Samiotiko, Roditiko, Kritiko, Sandorinio —"which makes the old man young," as he sometimes sang softly as he drank it. In other thinner bottles with long necks, which he called "camel-storks," he sealed his "cordial"—Barbaresou Koniak. Other liqueurs were kept in rose-coloured clay vessels like water-pipes with short necks. These bore exotic names: Kina-Kina, Rum, Cherry Brandy, Curaçao. One of them, the Jamaica, was dressed in fine straw which rustled when you touched it. In his cellar, clean and neat as a pharmacy, the bottles were arranged on shelves, some upright, some lying flat, others upside down, all according to the nectar they contained and my crazy uncle's theories about their preservation in good condition.

In a corner of the basement, in some small barrels—varnished and pretty like a drunkard's toys—the wine sat and matured until he bottled it, sealed it with his ring and laid it in its correct place.

Since his youth, my uncle had the habit of laying down old wines and spirits, as he'd always enjoyed taking a sip, now from one, now from another. Over time, and especially since the opening of the club, this had become a passion and his position as a connoisseur of wines and conscientious "President" of the club had become confused and he had become one of the best customers of his own *lokal*. He liked drinking a little of a series of his nectars at whatever hour of the twenty-four that the sudden desire overcame him, sometimes alone, sometimes with his friend the "repentant priest" or with one of his customers whom he happened to like at that moon. Because he was a little cantankerous, "like an old bachelor" as he said, without wishing to explain the vagaries of his character; and he continued to change with the moon, sometimes finding a comparative tranquility which he felt the need not to spoil with his hypochondria. Above all, he liked to drink slowly while reading a newspaper, a magazine or a book late at night—he slept very little. He had a passion for reading, which he made complete by selecting the right drink to accompany the subject matter, and so passed the heavy hours of sleeplessness, transforming them into an almost mystical intellectual and spiritual pleasure.

He'd given a nickname to every drink, characteristic of

the way it affected those who drank it. Often when he went to fetch the drinks, he would announce like a town-crier:

"The Good-Timer, the wine of Pasalimani, and The Free Spender, the Sandorinio will give us a happy high, if we're worthy of it."

Or he would announce like a master-of-ceremonies:

"I would like to inform you that the Koumandaria of Cyprus and 'the rhymester' Koniak have agreed to come into contact with your honoured gobs. Be careful not to be carried away by your enthusiasm."

Another time, he addressed a new member consolingly: "Our 'great lover' the Vassilios will bring with him his fellow-sufferers the 'lover boy' Kritiko and the 'caresser' Samiotiko."

Or again, looking a somewhat over-talkative customer directly in the eye and smiling: "Listen Vrassida, pardon me for asking, but won't you do us a favour and go and fetch us some of the exotic liquor to restore us a little?"

The club's single lounge contained only wooden, marble-topped tables and straw-bottomed upright chairs. On the four white-washed walls, at eye height, were hung a series of lithographs depicting mythological scenes from the Iliad and Odyssey, the history of Ancient Greece, the Old and New Testaments, the history of Ancient Rome and of Byzantium, the fall of Jerusalem to the crusaders and of Constantinople to Mehmet the Conqueror, the siege of

Vienna by Suleiman the Magnificent, Columbus among the Indians of America, Savonarola amidst the flames, scenes from the French Revolution with the guillotine and portraits of Robespierre and André Chénier—who my uncle especially loved both as a poet and because he had been born in The City, maybe at Fanar, the son of the Greek Elisavet Lomaki. Napoleon was shown watching Moscow burn.

The series ended with scenes from the Greek Revolution: the capture of Diakos, Kolokotronis's military camp in the Peloponnesos, a copy of Delacroix's painting of the slaughter of the Chiotes. The final lithograph was a coloured recreation of Agia Sophia, without its minarets and with a large Byzantine cross on the dome. A small picture-gallery of the history of the human race, which for the nostalgic patriot Hadji-Sofu-Thomas included, in a manner "painless" to the chauvinistic Turks, dramatic scenes from the struggle of the Greek People for their freedom.

Above the pictures, at a height reachable with an extended arm, a thick wooden shelf ran the length of the walls. On this, arranged in the correct order, were books, periodicals and newspapers bound together and tied with ribbon, a white label on each bundle bearing their names and dates. Newspapers which had been published in The City for many years: *Konstantinoupolis*, *Neologos*, *Tachidromos* and others. The periodicals included: *Bizantis*, *Propontis*, *Ekklisiastiki Aleithia* and several others. There were many books: historical, geographical, poetry and literature. All were placed in order without a single page missing. The old man kept them in good condition and only gave them to those he trusted; and then to be read in the Club and not taken home. For those who were not "conscientiously responsible," he got one of the more serious habitués to read out what they wished to learn. Sometimes he read to them himself and this was to their advantage as he knew how to read in such a way that they'd be able to understand well and not just get a rough idea. At the front of the shelves he had propped up newspapers, periodicals and books that were published in The City and had passed the Sultan's Censorship Board. Behind these legal publications were others printed in Greece: *Akropolis*, *Skrip*, *Kairoi*, *Rabagas*, Souris's *O Romios*, *Estia* and others which could get you into trouble in spy-ridden Turkey. Although my Uncle Thomas had had no systematic education, he loved reading and years of study had given him a sound knowledge of many subjects, especially history, both ancient and modern, which he lived with passionate interest. He was helped in this by his strong memory, which he called a "Phonographic Cylinder."

The glasses were kept in a sideboard, small ones for the spirits, medium-sized for the wine and the largest, and least used, for water. Beside the sideboard was an old-fashioned tap with a large marble basin under it in which my uncle washed both the glasses and himself. The drinking-water was kept in two large demijohns, bound in thick straw as far as their necks, which were brought full from springs famous for the quality of their water, such as "Taş Delen" and "Yakadjik." These springs gushed forth at idyllic spots around Constantinople, the ancient "Vassilevousa" or "Queen of Cities" of the boundless Byzantine State, the great capital of the old Ottoman Empire, enthroned between Asia and Europe, uniting East and West. Behind the sideboard, covering the full width of the room, hung heavy, faded Anatolian kilims. Behind them, a narrow space was formed at one end of which was the iconostasis and at the other the old man's bed, a mattress filled with dry seaweed and maize leaves laid on top of three planks supported by iron trestles. In an island chest made of cypress-wood, he kept his underwear with quinces placed among it to smell sweetly. He hung his few street-clothes on the wall, covered with a shawl. The heavy wooden table by his bed was always covered with books, periodicals and newspapers, along with his candleholder and a jug of water. This was his "bachelor's chamber," which resembled a Dervish's cell where reading, prayers and similar activities took place. But from a series of windows—lined up close together along the full width of the rear walls—his eye enjoyed, wherever it fell, shady glens, verdant valleys with cool streams, wooded hills where sun and shade played, and birds sang and leaves rustled, generously filling his ascetic abode with nature's rich beauty.

My uncle had never "entered the marriage market," as

he put it and I couldn't understand why. This fact and his somewhat unconventional life on the fringes of respectable society had given him the freedom not to transform his existence into a life-long shackling to a spouse, whom he would have to drag everywhere behind him like prisoners drag their chains. However, he "exercised his conjugal rights" unofficially and according to his wishes, sometimes with *derbederisses* or "free-living women," or with other races, or with the "Daughters of the Blessed Aphrodite," as he called the ancient Goddess with admiration. The only fillies he didn't dare mount were the Turkish ones, because, like the fox, he found them unsuitable for love-making under the threat of the Muslim fanaticism which hung like the sword of Damocles over those of other religions who dared to raise their eyes to "The Women of the Prophet."

Despite his trepidation regarding fatherhood—which, as he admitted, was due to his egoism—he loved children. He gave them sweets and simits, copybooks and coloured pens, pictures, transfers, books and icons, "to plant the seeds of knowledge in their minds," he said. He listened with affectionate interest to their complaints and little stories, always finding a way, with simple words, which spoke to their sensitive souls, to console them and calm them down. Sometimes saying they were right, at other times scolding them quietly in a joking way that made an impression on their childish imaginations and had a good influence on their malleable characters.

He liked me more than he did my brother and sister

and I really loved my Uncle Thomas because, of all the people I knew then he was the kindest and most just. I never saw him raise his hand to strike anybody, nor heard him shout. He spoke quietly in a warm and simple voice which gave you the courage to approach him and open your heart. At home my father screamed like a maniac and beat us for nothing, which was why I feared and hated him as much as I loved my uncle. Every morning on my way to school, I felt the need to pass by his Club, just to see him and say, "Good morning Hadji-Uncle," and that pleased him greatly. Then, there where he was sitting, he would place his two hands on my shoulders, look me deep in the eyes—as if seeking something—kiss me and with a smothered sigh whisper, "My boy." Then he would put a few coppers, a sweet or a picture into my hand, accompany me to the door of the Club, and in two words give me his blessing: "Sto kalo."

My uncle's Conversation Lounge was always frequented by the same people: "unregistered members of a non-existent Club," as he put it. Most of them were elderly householders, quiet, serious, soft-spoken, friends with each other and with the "Club President." But the period and depth of this friendship was decided by Old Thomas, dependent on how he judged each of them. Not only his fellow-villagers came to the Club, but also many others from surrounding parishes: pensioners, government employees, teachers, pharmacists, cantors, even lawyers and doctors and ordinary working men thirsting for knowledge. Several of these customers, who worked for English shipping companies—the most important ones in The City at the time—preferred to drink whiskey and gin, which they obtained duty-free from the English ships and supplied to the Club. Sofu-Thomas referred to them, as the "Anglo-Chiote gentlemen."

Some came to the Club to sip the old wines and exotic spirits. Others roosted in that simple and peaceful place—that "Oasis with the nectar"—to relax while reading a newspaper, a periodical or a book. But above all, they came to the Conversation Lounge to talk and to discuss whatever subject one or another of them might bring up; and for these descendants of the Byzantine windbags the subjects were many and various and became as mixed up as cherries on the stalk when they are poured from a basket. Parish matters became those of the whole Greek Community of The City, international political problems were confused with national ones, historical events became mixed up with philosophical and religious theories, scientific and geographical subjects took on vast dimensions. As the hour grew late, the discussion heated up and became more general to the point where all were gathered around a few tables, placed in lines opposite each other, and talked as in a session of "The Parliament of the Moons"—as Thomas called it—until after midnight. They talked quietly, sometimes spiritedly but never shouting, and heated as the discussion might grow, it never became a row.

Although Sofu-Thomas didn't speak much, he followed every discussion closely. When separate groups were chatting, he went slowly from one table to another, stood for a while listening carefully, and when he judged the moment suitable, said what he had to say, without being insistent, and moved on to the next table, although they would try to call him back to explain his point further. When a general discussion took place, he would sit a little apart listening attentively to all that was said as if taking notes in his memory. Sometimes he drew nearer, not to take part in the discussion but to stand behind someone who was beginning to shout or wave his arms excitedly and calm him with his silent presence.

Every time he spoke it was to give his opinion in a few words, always supported by clear evidence backed up with facts and dates. When somebody disagreed with him or doubted his words, he didn't get angry or repeat himself, but would go to the shelves and take down the relevant newspaper, periodical or book, find in there what was needed, bring it to the table and leave it open before whoever had disagreed with him, saying calmly but commandingly: "Read it." Then go and sit down as though uninterested. Again, when he was sitting apart talking quietly with a companion he had one ear on the general conversation and as soon as he heard an inaccuracy he would shout from where he was sitting: "Doctor, Look in *Neologos* for May, 1893 and you'll find the true facts about those fairy-stories you're spouting."

Despite his age, he remembered everything he had

read in the newspapers, periodicals and books that lay on the shelves of his Club. Those that interested him the most he had read twice, or more, so as to memorise whole extracts from the texts. Whenever anyone from his village or from other parishes to which the fame of Sofu-Thomas had spread had differences about political or historical subjects, they came to him for accurate information and the knowledge and evidence contained in the strange library of his Conversation Lounge.

Women sometimes came to the club. Not to settle at the tables and take part in the verbal diarrhoea of the males, but to obtain some old wine. Thomas would let wine leave the Club for only two reasons: he gave old women the famed Koumandaria of Cyprus for anointing those near death and the newborn; to others he provided strengthening wine to give to their ill relatives or their sickly children. However, he would only do this if he knew and respected the woman or one of her close family. Seemingly, he had very brief dealings with these women; though he did like to tease, in a way which pleased and amused them. Even if the jokes were a little spicy, they were clever and funny and he told them sweetly with an air of innocence, which is why the saucy wenches provoked the Old-Hadji both with their words and even more with their flirty ways.

One day, a notable and wealthy man, who was warden of the local church and a customer of the Club, sent his wife there to obtain some tonic wine for him as he was ill. Although she was more than mature, her hair was exaggeratedly curled and gaudily decorated with bows, ribbons, lace and braiding. Her throat, arms and fingers were laden with gold jewels which tinkled to her swaying walk and movements. Thomas gave her a sideways look, and as if continuing a conversation, said to a customer who was present: "By the way, it's time to cross yourself and make a pilgrimage to Saint Thekla the Kouvouklou."

The holy spring of Saint Thekla was in a small, green valley far away, where it bubbled, crystal-clear, from a spring which "the holy middlemen"—as Thomas called religious people—had fenced in with tall iron grill-work and a covering overhead like the cages of wild beasts at the circus. It was famous for curing headaches, eczema, womb problems and, though this was supposedly a secret, impotence. The faithful—Christians, Turks and others—came to drink the blessed waters, wet their heads with it and so be cured of all those afflictions. And, to be remembered there eternally, they tied to the railings of the Holy Thekla whatever they had with them: a ribbon, a braid, a chain, a hairpin, a comb or even a piece of material they tore from their clothes. All those motley little things swayed in the breeze of the valley giving a comical aspect to the miraculous spring of Saint Thekla the Kouvouklou.

Another time, a dry spinster, as flat in front as she was behind, came to the Club. She was the sister of a lawyer, a customer of the Club who, because of his weakness for her, couldn't get her to change her eccentric way of dressing or the silly way she flirted in order to attract a suitor. Thomas gave her some of the old wine she requested for her brother, but confronted by her coquetry, couldn't resist saying to the pharmacist who happened to be sitting there: "Manolaki, you forgot to bring me twenty parades worth of that powder which the beautiful women use on their mugs and I need to put on my itching arse."

Again, a well-made young woman, charming and healthy, whose beauty and body cried out to the men, "come here," entered the Club and requested some tonic wine for her husband.

"It would be better, my beauty," the Old Man answered smiling slyly, "if I gave you some anointing wine for him, as he's as old as I am, and you kept the tonic wine for whoever will take his place in the bridal chamber in the future."

He carried out his many kindnesses willingly and discretely as he wasn't conceited and didn't like people to speak about him. He gave money to the school, the community, and above all, to the poor. To the latter when they were recovering from illness, whatever their age, he sent old wine which a pharmacist friend of his had strengthened by adding quinquina. Although my uncle had the reputation of being cantankerous, he was respected by all who knew him well and they were many, thanks to his kindnesses. They all knew that, although he appeared indifferent and sometimes harsh, when it was necessary, he would be ready to help, quietly and with sympathy. In addition, he had the courage to openly express his opinion, correctly, justly and without prejudice, about anyone, Greek or Turk. These virtues and his wide knowledge had endowed my uncle with the triple name Sofu-Hadji-Thomas, a title respected by all, including the local "Zaptie" or policeman. The latter was a good-natured Kurd of average height who came regularly to the Club when it was quiet to drink some old wine or "tatlı leker"—"sweet liqueur," as he called it, with the Hadji-Baba, and in the Eastern way, exchange a few words full of meaning and calm.

The Club, with its outer shutters closed, would remain open past the appointed hour for as long as the discussion among the members and the President remained lively. The police never fined Thomas for this infringement, nor for any other, because, as he said, he had "taken a permit from the haberdasher," and the patrols which passed through the alleyways at night to make sure that nothing suspicious was going on and that all the shops were shut tight, had been instructed by the "Zaptie" to turn a blind eye to any transgressions by Sofu-Hadji-Thomas. As for the night-watchman, who was a Greek, he would beat a sign with his stick on the cobbles in front of the Club door and the Hadji would treat him to some tonic wine in good weather, or a warming spirit when it was cold, before he went on his way to guard the sleep of "the thieves who steal from each other," as he characterised the local "respectable" Greeks.

. . .

In all the years that the Club operated, only once was there big trouble. One evening, three Laconians who worked in the distilleries at Galata came over, theoretically to try the famed wines and spirits of Hadji-Thomas, but in reality to teach him a lesson. They had been sent by their bosses—also Laconians—because the fame of his Club's drinks was doing harm to their businesses and the old-grouch never bought any supplies from them. They entered the Club without a good evening to anyone, sprawled in chairs at one of the tables, clapped their hands thunderously and ordered:

"Bring us a little of all your so-called famous drinks old man, the customers are waiting to be served free at your coal-yard," and sniggered mockingly. They continued talking loudly making sarcastic comments about "the coffee man and his little café," as they sneeringly referred to Thomas and his club. The Hadji was furious and wanted to tell them to piss off, but controlled his rage and glumly went to fetch the drinks. He was helped with the serving by the youngest and most fearless of his customers. They didn't use a tray, but brought by hand three glasses and a single bottle of wine and placed them on the table, looking severely at the Laconians without speaking. The latter paid no attention to them, simply telling the old man to fetch them some meze and "the instruments" and without waiting for a reply began singing wildly and out of tune, while one of them got up and began to dance the *tsifteteli*, a belly dance. The provocation was crystal clear.

Two or three of those present wanted to order the

insolent newcomers to behave themselves, but Old-Thomas, like a man who knows his responsibilities, wanted to avoid the consequences and stopped them. He went over alone to the Laconians and explained in a soft but stern voice that what they wanted was not available at the Club. He added that singing and dancing were not allowed and advised them to sit quietly like the other customers. The Laconians indicated that the tapster's words didn't please them and abused him horribly. Again controlling his rage, Hadji-Thomas told them where the best taverna in the village was and advised them to go there, where they would find whatever their hearts desired—drinks, food, music—and they could sing and dance as much as they liked. This time the Laconians pretended they were deeply insulted because the "old coffee-man" was throwing them out and began to swear and threaten him. This brought all customers in the Club to their feet. They joined in the row and formed a threatening circle round the three Laconians, who were obliged to leave, cursing as they went and swearing to get revenge on the Club, the owner, the customers and the whole village.

They couldn't swallow their failure, and a few evenings later six Laconians set out from Galata with the intention of smashing up the Club and so get revenge on the Club President and his fellow villagers for the insult they had suffered. However, some Kephalonians from the neighbouring parish—who worked as longshoremen on the quay at Galata and hung out at the Laconian distilleries—got wind of the rough-necks' plans and on the evening in question five or six of them went early to the Club and sat there discretely without saying a word. Old Thomas was puzzled by the sudden appearance of so many of them, but because he knew they were good and worthy lads, who sometimes worked at the transportation of his wines, he greeted them warmly, even though he was a little uneasy and smelt that something might be up. In a little while the six Laconians arrived. The three original ones with another three hard nuts. They burst in like a mob, in the style of "here we are!", and without even a greeting, loudly pulled two tables together, as well as a heap of chairs on which they sprawled insolently, some occupying two, others three. They shouted and gawked around them as if the Club was some cheap wine house which they'd paid to take over for their own use, without considering the other customers. Sofu-Thomas realised why they had come. Shaken and uneasy, he tried to think of a way to get rid of these undesirables and forestall big trouble. The Kephalonians, who were watching developments, signalled to each other to be ready for action, but remained still. The Laconians—after insultingly ordering the "old tapster" and his lads to bring them a lot of his so-called good wines and spirits along with plenty of mezes—began to loudly boast about their obscene feats and to make insulting remarks about the Club and the village, guffawing shamelessly.

Suddenly, a thunderous voice was heard from the Kephalonians: "You there! We can hear you. This is a classy establishment. Not some Laconian factory in Galata..."

The Laconians answered back like a bunch of tough-guys, saying they'd enjoy themselves by spending their money however they liked and anyone who didn't like it could piss off if he didn't want to be thrown out like stale bread. Two of them stood up ready for a fight, but they weren't quick enough. The Kephalonians pulled out their *stropia*—a form of lead weighted black-jack bound around with wire—and fell on the Laconians. Tables were overturned, marble tops broken, chairs smashed, glasses shattered. Swearing, grunts, the sound of the blows of the black-jacks and whatever else came to hand accompanied the loud crashing of breaking objects. Two or three customers ran and closed the shutters so the locals and passers-by wouldn't gather outside the Club and so attract the attention of the police and gendarmes. Some customers wanted to join in on the battle and help the Kephalonians, but Old-Thomas forbade them commandingly. They stood aside and watched with interest and almost with admiration the fighters and their clever moves, without worrying about the damage. The Laconians took the beating of their lives and left in disarray, leaving some of their armoury in the hands of the victors: a heavy studded leather belt, a stiletto and a black-jack. Thomas later hung them on the walls as trophies among the pictures of the Greek and French revolutions. The damage wasn't very great as the Old Man, with the assistance of the young customer who had helped him during the previous clash with the Laconians, had deliberately delayed serving the drinks.

The Kephalonians helped some customers to clean up the battle-field and restore anything unbroken to its rightful place; then returned to their table as if nothing had happened. Sofu-Hadji-Thomas didn't know how to thank them. Pale, he embraced one of them, hugged him to his chest, held his head between his two hands and without saying a word, kissed him on the forehead; he who hadn't even kissed his dead father. All those who were in the Club gathered round the victors, chatted with them, bought them drinks, thanked them and discussed the battle, commenting sarcastically on the run-away pseudo tough-guys. The Kephalonians said modestly that they'd only done their duty out of respect for Uncle-Thomas and after a while left quietly, assuring my uncle they'd always be at his side in time of need. The Laconians never returned. However, the event was learned of at Galata and two of their fellow-countrymen—among the most important of the distillers of fine liqueurs who supplied Thomas—came and sought his understanding and forgiveness for what had been done by the jackals, who didn't know how worthy of respect Sofu-Hadji-Thomas was. They toasted him with the French cognac they had brought as a gift; Martell three-star, knowing that the old-connoisseur preferred it above all others, since he said of it: "By drinking the cordial Martell, you bring to life what's below the navel."

. . .

My uncle Hadji-Thomas died at over eighty. Suddenly, of apoplexy as he had wished for himself, saying: "I don't want the old dotard Charon to come for me. I want to be taken by the good Lady Euthanasia."

And I, young as I was when I heard those words, would ask myself who this Lady was, so I could go and beg her not to take my uncle. God rest his soul. I owe many of my gifts and talents to him. With his knowledge and his wise words he opened my eyes and broadened my mind, helped me to distinguish between right and wrong, the beautiful and the ugly, and showed me how to enjoy life. What I took from his thoughts and ways is rooted in my soul and has accompanied me throughout life to the point where I've felt his presence as a support long after his death. Thanks to his freedom of thought, which understood the importance of good wine and sweet liqueurs to a man's physical and mental health, he gave me to try, from an early age—naturally in small amounts—now one and now another of the old wines and spirits with exotic names which he kept in the cellar of his Club. Inexperienced in life, I took great pride in this and over time good drink became a pleasant personal institution that I enjoyed fully for many years, sometimes with wisdom, sometimes carelessly when I lived the life of an idle drinker. My life, with its entanglements, caused me to see my beloved uncle less often than I would have liked; but whenever the twists of those loose-living times permitted I went to find him at the Club during the hours when he was all alone. Then we enjoyed each other's company with heartfelt pleasure. We sat opposite each other, drank "one for me, one for you," from whatever type of drink he selected and I waited for him to say, as when I was young:

"Naklet — tell me, Stavri, my child..."

And, simply and humbly, I would go over all my adventures hiding nothing from him, even the worst things I'd done. He'd listen calmly, his eyes caressing me, and when I happened to stop he'd whisper:

"Go on Stavro, I'm old now and everything you're telling me about yourself I'll take with me when my eyes close. I've got no one else in the world now to give me anything."

And his affectionate look would fill my soul with emotions I felt at no other time. Every time he heard about a really indecent or recklessly dangerous action of mine, he would say quietly and confidentially: "Try everything in life Stavro, yes everything, but don't forget, all in moderation."

Wise words he knew the truth of from his studies and from his experience of life that he had explained to me when I was young, and even later when I was all grown up.

In his will, beautifully written in his own hand, he named three executors: a lawyer of about his age—retired, but still very bright and a bit of a womaniser—his friend the "repentant priest," and me. The three of us were very sad to carry out this melancholic duty, but found a little consolation in drinking some of the dear departed's wines in his memory. He left nothing to any of his friends or relations; only mementoes for each of the three of us: the two old icons and the silver candle-stick to the "repentant priest," a holy book to the old lawyer—the whoremonger—and his agate ring to me. His clothes, the tables and chairs and the Club's other household goods were divided, according to his wishes, amongst the poor of the parish. The newspapers, periodicals, books and lithographs were left to the school library. From his cellar, he ordered that the exotic liqueurs be divided amongst the elderly poor of the parish "so they can sweeten their souls before they give them up to The Lord and before they reach the fasting and dryness of Paradise." He wrote that the tonic wines be given to sickly children and to any lads among the local artisans or from the fire-brigade who were recovering from illness. The Koumandaria of Cyprus was to be divided among the old women, the mid-wives and the layers-out of the dead, to be used for anointing. He was certain that those God-fearing women would respect his wishes and save that famous wine as something to be used only for holy rituals and not drink it for their own pleasure as the church-goers would. But before these terms were carried out, he demanded that wines and spirits be drunk at his memorial service.

Just enough money was found at the Club to carry out his funeral as he desired, with early-Christian simplicity. The procession was led by a strong young fellow carrying the black cross from the un-nailing of Jesus on Good Friday. He was followed by two lads, each with a black candle in his hand which the Hadji had brought from Jerusalem. There was one priest in the procession—as there had to be, even though the departed would have done without—and he wore only a single stole over his robe. Then came the coffin containing the dead Sofu-Thomas wrapped in the white shroud of a Hadji. He was carried by his friends and the regulars at the Club. Young, middle-aged and old changing places every so often. Only the "repentant priest"—silent and inconsolable, his eyes bright with tears and fixed on his dead friend—refused to give up his place and bore the front of the coffin from the moment that the remains were lifted until the moment they were lowered into the tomb. Not even I who loved my uncle so could persuade him to leave that sad position.

As my late uncle had wished, his friends the *psaltes*, or cantors, had come from the two local parishes along with their bass-droners and choir-boys. They accompanied the dead Hadji-Thomas the whole way, one group on the right, the other on the left; sometimes all together, sometimes separately, they chanted sorrowfully and heartrendingly for the death of a much loved person. Behind the coffin followed all classes of people from the village and from surrounding parishes. Among them, standing out for their deep grief, were the regulars at the Club who as well as their "President" had lost the lively oasis of their lonely lives. They buried him as he had requested in his will, apart from the family tomb. Over him is laid flat a simple, black, iron cross and written on it the words: SOFU-HADJI-THOMAS 1814–1896.

Nine days later, his memorial service was attended by many from the village and from other parishes. Friends, people who knew him, people who hadn't known him, all collected at the cemetery; some in respect for his memory, others to sample for the final time—and some for the first time—his old wines and liquors. The faithful from the Conversation Lounge crowded tightly round his grave and drank the wine of Sofu-Hadji-Thomas for the last time, after first pouring a little onto his newly made grave and saying from the depths of their hearts: "God rest his soul."

THIRTEEN

Mousiou-Mamourithras

He must have been around fifty, born and bred in Tatavla. His godfather, who had a little education and had read the lesson in the church of the Metochi of Panagios Taphos in Athens, baptised him with two names: one pagan, Alcibiades, the other Christian, Ananias. His father's family name was Karamarsikis, because it seems that all his ancestors were, like him, slightly built and sallow complexioned. This surname however, did not please Alcibiades-Ananias and he changed it to Mavroeididis. He spoke in a deliberately simple, sweet voice, as though reading the "Holy Word," and was very polite in a ceremonious way and also welcoming and obliging. His clothes and his house were neat and tidy; all in all, he was a respectable and god-fearing person, a "Mousious." He attended church regularly both at festivals and on Sundays and assisted the cantors and deacons, a perfect *mamourithras*. So, his fellow parishioners named him

"Mousiou-Mamourithras," though he insisted they call him "Mousiou-Mavroeididis." Both his nickname and his double-barrelled name were uncommon and hard to remember and were often forgotten; not however by him, and he used them judiciously whenever necessity called.

He had a hard bowler hat, a little the worse for wear, like his small, pointed head with its thinning silver hair, but he wore it as proudly as a crown. Around his long and wrinkled neck was a hard collar and a faded cherry-coloured bowtie. His black suit was shiny with wear. He only fastened the top two buttons of his tight-waisted jacket in order to show off his spotted brown waistcoat, his gold-plated chain with its nickel watch and the false, blue turquoise stone which hung as a charm to ward off the evil eye. His trousers narrowed at the bottom and fell over his wrinkled, shiny, pointed boots. He trimmed his curved moustache to make his bony face look younger. Two small, dark eyes shone uneasily and inquisitively, you'd think they were trying to join with his thick eyebrows and long nose to escape from his large, pointed ears like bats' wings. In the street he always carried a thin, black walking stick with a curved silver handle and in his other hand a small bag like a doctor's.

By profession he was a *mousamadjis*—he covered floors with oilcloth and carpets. As a capable and renowned craftsman, he worked in the houses of the rich, the mansions of pashas and in banks. In his bag, as well as the tools of his trade, a hammer, pincers and special knives, he carried *katsakiko*—a black market tobacco.

As an experienced "Katsakji" he carried a number of packets large and small, of the "Regie de Tabacs de L'Empire Ottoman"; in theory an Ottoman monopoly, but which was actually in the hands of foreign exploiters. He kept these in good condition so they always looked new. Inside them he placed smuggled tobacco of exactly the same weight as written on the packet and sealed it with the ribbon of the "Regie," so expertly placed as to seem brand new. For his customers, he unstuck the ribbon carefully and emptied the sweet-smelling tobacco. It was of a special blend cut with his own hands and ensured him a regular clientele. That's how he sold his black-market tobacco, and if it happened that the packets were discovered in his bag by any official, he got away with it because of his shabby appearance and by whining that he'd ended up selling tobacco in the streets to support his large family in these difficult days, as his craft only gave him work in the wintertime. As for the empty packets, he explained that he kept them for his children to play with and so learn the trade of a grocer or small shopkeeper.

The black marketeers brought the bales of tobacco by night to the gulley at the foot of the hill below the village not far from Mr Ananias's house, and hid it in hollows in the ground which they covered with branches and greenery. From there, one by one, they brought them late at night to Mr Alcibiades's house; a three-storied, wooden building set among others, all black as mummies with age and leaning together like a bunch of maimed people supporting each other. You could only tell them apart by the odd detail: curtains, doors, flowers and sometimes by the number, if they had one, written in Turkish or European figures. But even that wasn't sure as every now and again Mr Ananias exchanged his number with that of another house when a search by the authorities was due. At the front of his house facing the road was a small yard, and at the rear a long, narrow garden led down to the bottom of the hill and a dirt-road which ran beside the gulley.

The Police Drug Squad suspected that Mousiou-Mamourithras was a black-marketeer, but he had a thousand and two ways of out-smarting them. He was helped in this by his many names, which he knew how to use to confuse them and cover his traces and they never managed to catch him in the act. Apart from that, he always made sure to be on good terms with the local police officers and the ordinary patrol men and regularly gave them small amounts of *bakshish*, so they looked on him as an honest man and a quiet householder. If any of them became difficult and couldn't be controlled in a soft way, Mamourithras had other ways of making them see reason. He gave abundant supplies of his best blend tobacco to the most notorious *daïdes* and they were always ready to help him out. They went into action and in a quiet but threatening way made the difficult policeman understand that he should leave the poor man in peace. No copper dared to fall-out with those fearless men, who were also involved in contraband of every type.

That's how Mousiou-Mamourithras had his protection

and defence well organised. Also, since the young hangers-on of the *daïdes* and every type of *rebetis* got their share of the carpet fitter's black-market tobacco—even if of lower quality—they were ready to tip him off when they got wind of any police approaching. Then, any tobacco that Mr Mavroeididis had in his house disappeared immediately. As the houses were joined together it was easy to communicate between them over the roofs, which for reasons of economy had no partition walls between them. So as soon as the patrols began to search one house, the bales of tobacco were in another in the next neighbourhood, usually without the householder having any idea of what was happening on his roof.

In Mr Ananias's front yard was a pool, quite large and deep. He filled it with rainwater which he used to water the vegetables in the large garden that sloped downwards at the rear of the house. Over time the water in this pool became green and attracted all kinds of bugs and mosquitoes, which annoyed Mr Alcibiades and his family, particularly in the summertime. Mr Mavroeididis regularly read newspapers, *The Neologos* and *The Constantinople*, which he picked up from the offices he went to in the course of his work as a carpet-layer and had enough knowledge to fear catching fevers and other diseases from the dirty water. He wanted to empty the pool but couldn't bear to spend the money needed. He wasn't able to do it himself as he couldn't spare the time from his other occupations, his wife was sickly and his children still too young, the oldest was just ten. He couldn't fall back on the *daïdes* or their apprentices for such a chore. For the former it would be unseemly and the latter he would have to pay, and Mousiou-Mamourithras loved money and his principle was never to spend it without a serious reason. He cudgelled his brains to think of a way of getting the work done free. Keeping an eye on the movements of the police patrols, he noticed that from time to time they chatted to his children and tried to wheedle information from them. The kids, apart from knowing nothing about their father's work, had been instructed by him, with the threat that he'd cut out their tongues with his knife, to never say a word to anyone about what went on in the house.

From time to time, the authorities decided to systematically and harshly hunt down the tobacco black marketeers. The newspapers wrote of the terrible penalties which would be imposed for the "crime," as they called it, and the rewards that would be given to those who helped the police to track down the smugglers. Mr Alcibiades–Ananias instantly took extra precautions but continued his work as both a carpet-layer and a black marketeer as before. Work is work. The patrols watched Mousiou-Mamourithras more closely than ever, their suspicions made stronger by his behaviour; and one day they decided to make a sudden search of his home. However, he had made his plans some time before and expected their visit. Indeed, he made preparations to receive them and told his children, "When the coppers come, don't be scared. You can ask them for sweets. They'll give them to you. They're good people. And when they ask you where 'Baba-Effendi' hides his tobacco tools, say they're in the pool." And that's what happened.

As soon as the police heard what the children said, they immediately called for some labourers and put them to work emptying the pool. To make things quicker, the cops themselves even took part in the work, sure that this time they would catch the big fish. The tools for tobacco cutting would be a victory trophy for them. Especially the *chavani*, a small, round trough made of a single piece of wood with a smooth, raised platform in the middle on which the tobacco was finely cut with a curved knife attached to the edge. The tobacco fell from the platform into the trough and was easily collected.

Whenever the police uncovered a *chavani* they returned it triumphantly to the "Regie" and received a large *bakshish* in golden Turkish liras. The guilty black marketer was treated as a serious criminal and was sent to prison or into exile, as well as having to pay a heavy fine for "depriving the Ottoman state of legitimate income"; that is to say depriving the greedy foreign interests who held the tobacco monopoly. If he was unable to pay the fine, all his assets, including his children's clothes, would be confiscated and put up for auction. If the police only found smuggled tobacco, the punishments were less and the smuggler got off fairly lightly. The *chavani* was the greatest evidence of guilt and so "the coppers made every effort to empty the pool as fast as possible in order to find it," as Mr Ananias chortled later.

His children, along with others from the neighbourhood had a great time. They played with the water, made little pools, rivers, ports with bridges, sailed their boats made of wood and paper, had naval battles. Mr Mavroeididis, who the police believed was absent, was inside his house and watched the emptying joyfully from behind the curtains of a second-floor window. Although the policemen thrust their hands into the sludge at the bottom of the now emptied pool to find the longed-for trophy, they found nothing. So they could bring no charges against Mousiou-Mamourithras. Just the opposite, he was able to complain of "Disturbance of Family Peace," with unpleasant consequences for the coppers. Above all, he had made fools of them and their incompetence as they had found neither *chavani* nor tobacco and had wasted money on emptying the pool; so damaging the prestige of both the Police Authorities and the "Regie." Although furious at their set-back, the coppers confined themselves to swearing at each other and left shame-faced, shouting threats at the invisible smuggler as they went. They didn't even consider telling off the children as they knew their favourite game in such circumstances was throwing stones. The kids, seeing the coppers arguing among themselves, had moved away and had formed a circle as if holding positions in readiness for a row. So, Mr Alcibiades-Ananias-Mavroeididis got his pool cleaned out and no longer had to fear the fevers and paroxysms brought on by the bugs and mosquitoes.

On another occasion, the Honoured Governor of The City had ordered through a firman stamped with the Sultan's emblem that none of the many animals which grazed in the valleys around Feriköy be allowed to pass in herds through the central streets on their way to the slaughter houses, which were scattered around the great capital. Some herdsmen then decided to use as a short cut the dirt-road which ran below the village hill and past the bottom of Mr Alcibiades-Ananias's vegetable garden. It wasn't a good road, but suitable for livestock. From then on, whole herds of cattle and other animals passed at night from the fields to the slaughter houses and in the opposite direction from Kasımpaşa, where they were unloaded from boats and driven to Vourgarika, the Bulgarian neighbourhood beyond Bomonti, where the biggest and most colourful livestock market of the City, that great Eastern metropolis, took place on European soil. As they passed by there was tremendous din from their feet and mooing and baaing. The dust they raised was carried by the wind to the houses high above and made the "delicate" Mrs Mavroeididi cough, and in addition, the microbes it contained were dangerous for the growing children's health. Mr Alcibiades-Ananias was very upset by all this and was losing his sleep worrying. He believed that every wrong action had its price, and someone would have to be punished for this, someone would have to pay.

He discussed the matter with a resourceful neighbour, Ele of Doudou, who knew something about dealing with animals, and with another clever fellow, Sarı Yiovan or "Blond Yianni," a Bulgarian butcher whose shop had been closed by the police because he sold bad meat. The three of them put a new scheme into action which lasted quite some time. When a herd passed at night, one of them, Ele of Doudou, opened the gate at the bottom of the garden and another, Sarı Yiovan, who was waiting outside tight up against the garden wall, pushed a calf, or even a full-grown steer inside. The herdsmen didn't get wind of it as they walked at either the front or rear of the long herd which made its way noisily down the narrow dirt road. As soon as the animal was inside, Ele stuffed a large bunch of fresh hay into its mouth to keep it quiet and pulled it up the garden by the horns. Sarı Yiovan pushed it gently but firmly from behind, both of them making noises which calm and command animals. Keeping the animal well supplied with fodder, they guided it to a shed high up in the garden where the Boss, Mr Alcibiades-Ananias-Mavroeididis, was waiting. Before his eyes the other two slaughtered the animal, cleaned it, skinned it and under his instructions, cut it into three equal portions. He kept the head, the tripe and the feet for his family; strength-giving food for the sickly Mavroeididis breed. Dawn found them ready, the work all done, the shed cleared of blood, the inedible parts spread at the roots of the trees for fertiliser and the bloody water used to water the vegetables.

The two helpers had no families to care for and sold their portions to the itinerant Albanian butchers. Sometimes, out of nostalgia for his old trade, Sarı Yiovan would put a rough wooden table on his head, with the meat on top covered with a white, fly-covered cloth, and with Ele of Doudou by his side, pass through the poor neighbourhoods shouting proudly, "Fine meat, ore! Fresh, bre!"

He sold it cheaper than the other street-butchers and more generously weighed, for the good of his soul. The poor people bought it willingly and considered it unjust that the *asikis* or fine-fellow Ele was called a lazy-bones and that the police hounded the Bulgarian, such a good-hearted person. May God give them good-times and let their parents rest in peace.

Mr Mavroeididis kept most of his share for the family to eat fresh, or to make *soutzoukakia* and *kavourma*; although, he put aside a few good pieces for gifts to friends whom he wanted to be obligated to him. He used some lean bits for a meze to accompany his evening ouzo. Then he would take pleasure in sitting with friends by the pool and enjoying its cool, while goldfish swam in the clean water and for their meze ate the bugs and the "bearers of malarial fever."

Glossary

Andrikos = a tender way to say the name Andris/Andreas

arkadaşlar (turk.) = friends, partners

asikis (turk: aşık) = 1. a lover 2. a dashing, strapping man, 3. A wandering bard/poet

aşure (ashure) = a dessert porridge that is made of a mixture consisting of grains, fruits, dried fruits and nuts

Ay-Yiorgi = Saint George (Greek colloquial)

azizim (turk.) – my dear friend

baba = 1. father 2. a respectful way of addressing an old man

bakshish (turk: bahşiş) = a tip, a gratuity payment, a small amount of money for services rendered

barba = uncle

besliki (turk: beşlik) = a "fiver," a five cent coin

bey (turk.) = sir, mister

bidets-ala-franga = literally "bidets in the French style," a washbasin

binedes = wash-basins

bre, ore = Greek exclamatory sounds

bülbül (turk.) = nightingale (also the place-name Bülbül Dere)

çalgılar (turk.) = musical instruments

çarşı (turk.) = marketplace, a bazaar

chavani = mortar (turk: havan)

daïliki = the practice of bravado and toughness

daïs, (pl.) *daïdes* = street tough, a bully, hard-man

dalga (turk.) = literally "wave," used to describe the high from smoking hashish

deniz kataif or *deniz kadayıf* (turk.) = "sea-noodles" or "sweet-seaweeds"

derbederissa, (pl.) *derbederisses* (turk: derbeder) = free-spirited, independent, bohemian woman

dere (turk.) = 1. brook, stream or creek. 2. valley

dokmetzis, (pl.) *dokmetzides* (turk: dökmeci) = a foundry worker

dragoman = interpreter, translator, guide

gazel, (pl.) *gazeller* = Turkish song in the Ottoman music tradition

hadji (turk: hacı) = pilgrim either to Jerusalem or Mecca

hajmali = a talisman

hamal (turk.) = a porter who carries loads on his back, figuratively a common, coarse fellow

han (turk.) = an Ottoman Turkish building that consisted of cells arranged around a courtyard, and included places for sleeping, stables, storage and wholesale activities

hasap (turk: kasap) = butcher

hasiklis, (pl.) *hasiklides* = hash-smoker

kabadayı (turk.) = loosely: a "tough guy," an underworld figure

kaltak (turk.) = slang for "whore" or "bitch"

karamanlis (turk: Karamanlı) = a Greek from Central Anatolia

karsilamas, (pl.) *karsilamades* (turk: karşılama) = a couple folk dance with a 9/8 meter

kavourma (turk: kavurma) = a cooked/preserved meat used in Turkish cuisine as well as other Ottoman ethnic groups *kerhane* (turk.) = house of ill repute, a brothel

kerhanedzou (turk: kerhaneci kadın) = the "patrona," the madam of the brothel

kior (turk: kör) = blind

kısmet (turk.) = fate or destiny, in Islam "the will of Allah"

komiseris (turk: komiser) = head of the police

koumbaros, (pl.) *koumbari* = best man at a wedding

külhanbeyi (turk.) = a roughian, a tough guy, a *mangas*

laterna = a barrel-organ

lecha = woman from Poland

levantinika = language spoken by the Levantines of the Ottoman Empire

levendissa = fine, upstanding, brave woman

lokal = the place of activity, or the centre of an association (Turkish use of the French word: locale)

lokum = the sweet "Turkish delight"

loulas = the bowl of a hookah, or a nargile

manedes = solo vocal improvisations based on Ottoman musical modes

mangas = a "tough guy"

mastoras = chief artisan

meraklis, (pl.) *meraklides* = passionate, enthusiast, devotee, good-timer

merhaba (turk.) = "hello" in Turkish

merhametli (turk.) = compassionate, merciful or kind-hearted one

metaliki (turk: metelik) = two "fivers," or two five-cent coins

Metochi of Panagios Taphos = Small church belonging to the Jerusalem

Orthodox Patriarchate, situated in other cities (like Constantinople and Athens)

mousiou = mister (a variant of the French word "monsieur" in the Greek and Turkish language of old Constantinople)

nargiles = a hookah

odjak (turk: ocak) = a hearth

omphalos = navel, umbilicus, the "centre"

ore, bre = Greek exclamatory sounds

pivatianos = adjective for someone whose origin was the town of Epivates (today: Selimpaşa) in Eastern Thrace

rakı = Turkish drink similar to the Greek ouzo

rebetis = member of the *rebetiko* subculture, with connotations of vagrancy, profligacy and being a layabout

sala = a salon, a hall, a large living area, or a reception room

sokak (turk.) = street

Souris Yeorgios (1852-1919) = satirical poet of modern Greece

soutzoukakia = also known as "Smyrnan meatballs," a Greek and Turkish dish of meatballs in thick tomato sauce

sto kalo = a Greek wish given to someone who leaves, meaning "blessed be your way"

teke (turk: tekke) = a place where hashish can be bought and consumed at leisure. Originally a dervish or Sufi lodge

tsardi (turk: çardak) = pergola, (metaphorically: a house).

tsifteteli = a kind of "belly dance" or more accurately a dance in 2/4 meter common amongst Balkan and Anatolian peoples, usually danced by women and effeminate men

tsipouro = a mainland Greek word for raki, a drink of distilled alcohol.

yabandji (turk: yabancı) = stranger, foreigner

yavrum, (pl.) *yavrumlar* = a figurative expression: "my child" or "my children". (Note: the correct form of this word in Turkish is "yavrularım". Here it is written as Tzelepis rendered it).

yeia sas = way of greeting in Greek, meaning "health to you"

zeïbekiko = a Greek folk dance which takes its name from the *Zeybek* nomads of Western Anatolia, usually danced in an improvised way by solitary performers

Place Names

The following list is a selection of place names mentioned in the book.

Fanar = Quarter midway up the Golden Horn within the district of Fatih. In Turkish *Fener*, from the Greek word meaning a streetlight or lantern.

Feriköy = Quarter adjacent to Sinemköy in Kurtuluş/Tatavla.

Fındıklı = Quarter next to the Galata port in Istanbul.

Galata = A central part of the port of Istanbul, on the Beyoğlu section of the city.

Great Street of Pera = Street that corresponds to today's Istiklal avenue.

Gümüşsuyu = Quarter on the slope between Taksim hill and Kabataş port.

Kayit Hane (*Kâğıthane*) = District at the very end of the Golden Horn.

Kayseri = City in Central Anatolia (Cappadocia), in ancient times called Caesaria.

Kondoskali = The Greek name of the quarter Kumkapı in Istanbul.

Mısır Çarşı = The Spices Bazar in Eminonu, Istanbul.

Pera = The Greek name for the district called in Turkish: Beyoğlu

Sakız-Ağaç = Name of a street in Beyoğlu, literally meaning "mastic tree."

Scutari = The Greek name for Üsküdar, on the Asian coast of Istanbul.

Sinemköy = Quarter adjacent to Kurtuluş/Tatavla.

Stavrodromi = Literally means the "crossroads." It is the name once used by the Greek community of Istanbul for the area known as Beyoğlu or Pera. It refers to the crossroad of Galatasaray which is situated at the centre of this area.

Tatavla = The district named Kurtuluş in Turkish.

Tinos = Greek island, one of the Cyclades, in the Aegean Sea. Popular among Orthodox Greeks for its miraculous Virgin Mary monastery and church.

Yeni Şehir = The district between Tarlabaşı (Taksim) and Kurtuluş.

Glossary prepared by Niki Stavridi and Michael Alexandratos

Photograph of Panos N. Tzelepis, c. late 1950s
Archive of Michalis Stafilas.

The architect and writer Panos N. Tzelepis was born in Constantinople (Istanbul) in 1894, the son of Nikolis Tzelepis, a renowned master builder. In 1915 the family moved to Athens, and there Tzelepis studied painting and sculpture at the School of Fine Arts, later moving on to Paris where he studied architecture at the École Spéciale d'Architecture.

On his return to Athens in 1922 he first engaged in graphic design work. In the two decades that followed, Tzelepis established himself as one of the foremost representatives of modernist architecture in Greece.

At the end of World War Two he moved to Paris, where besides working as an architect he also published his first book in French in 1947, which was a study of architecture for children.

He later returned to Greece in 1956, where he dedicated himself mainly to writing.

During the 1930s, Tzelepis recorded the memories of his older relative Stavris, who was a "retired" kabadayı (tough guy) from Constantinople.

Later he published these memoirs in Athens in two volumes, the first in 1965, titled *In the Time of the Sultans* and the second in 1971 under the title *The Story of a Daïs*. Tzelepis died in Athens in 1976.

Books by Panos N. Tzelepis

Villages d'Enfants (Children's Villages), Paris: Edition A. Morancé, 1947.

L'Architecture Populaire en Gréce (Popular Architecture of Greece), Paris: Edition A. Morancé, 1952.

Στον καιρό των Σουλτάνων (In the Time of the Sultans), Athens: self-published, 1965. Re-published in 2003, Trochalia editions.

Τραγούδι που δεν τελειώνει – νοσταλγικά δίστιχα (The Song That Never Ends – Nostalgic Verses), Athens, 1966.

Λαϊκή ελληνική αρχιτεκτονική (Greek Popular Architecture), Athens, 1971. Re-published in 1999, Themelio editions.

Ένας νταής (The Story of a Daïs), Athens: self-published, 1971.

About the Translator

Charles Howard, a painter, researcher and archiver of Greek *rebetiko* music, was born in London in 1936. He has lived in Greece for over forty years and has compiled, edited, translated and annotated 22 compilations of *rebetiko* music for the Heritage, Rounder and JSP record labels in England and the U.S.A. *In the Time of the Sultans* is his first book-length translation work. He currently lives in Athens.

www.ingramcontent.com/pod-product-compliance
Lightning Source LLC
Chambersburg PA
CBHW070010120726
47909CB00003B/866

* 9 7 8 0 6 4 6 8 3 9 5 9 2 *